'It *was* a palace, and is now a hospital.' Philippe suddenly appeared, materialising from within the depths of the monumental building. '"The Palace of Love Divine", built by a sultan in the fourteenth century, and so called because legend has it that he had an insatiable appetite for women.'

Harriet stared at him. It wasn't her imagination, there was definitely an undertone of mocking sensuality in his voice.

It reeked of chauvinism and annoyed her. 'How interesting,' she said icily. 'The sultan would have quite a shock if he came back now. Finding the place full of sick patients, looked after and organised by emancipated western women.'

Ann Jennings has been married for thirty-two years and worked in a hospital for fourteen years—accounting for the technicalities accurately described in her hospital romances. Her son is a doctor and often provides her with amusing tidbits of information. Hospitals are romantic places, she maintains, romance blossoms where two people share a common interest.

Previous Titles
SURGEON ASHORE
SOLD TO THE SURGEON
REALLY, DOCTOR!
NURSE ON LOAN

NEW BEGINNINGS

BY
ANN JENNINGS

MILLS & BOON LIMITED
ETON HOUSE 18-24 PARADISE ROAD
RICHMOND SURREY TW9 1SR

All the characters in this book have no existence outside the imagination of the Author, and have no relation whatsoever to anyone bearing the same name or names. They are not even distantly inspired by any individual known or unknown to the Author, and all the incidents are pure invention.

All Rights Reserved. The text of this publication or any part thereof may not be reproduced or transmitted in any form or by any means, electronic or mechanical, including photocopying, recording, storage in an information retrieval system, or otherwise, without the written permission of the publisher.

This book is sold subject to the condition that it shall not, by way of trade or otherwise, be lent, resold, hired out or otherwise circulated without the prior consent of the publisher in any form of binding or cover other than that in which it is published and without a similar condition including this condition being imposed on the subsequent purchaser.

First published in Great Britain 1989 by Mills & Boon Limited

© Ann Jennings 1989

*Australian copyright 1989
Philippine copyright 1989
This edition 1989*

ISBN 0 263 76511 3

*Set in Palacio 11 on 12½ pt.
03-8908-41235*

Typeset in Great Britain by JCL Graphics, Bristol

Made and Printed in Great Britain

CHAPTER ONE

'EXCUSE me, *please!*' Exasperated at the interruption, Harriet's voice was sharper than she had intended. But the last thing she needed at that particular moment was to cannon into a very solid form.

'I do beg your pardon,' a deep voice said apologetically, as a tall man stepped out of the way. He smiled, only to be rewarded by a withering glance from Harriet.

Really, some people, she thought crossly, you'd think they would have enough sense not to stand right outside operating theatre swing doors!

As the porters backed the trolley out of the operating theatre, Harriet squeezed through the narrow gap at the side as best she could. Allowing herself one more irate glower at the cause of the collision, she then concentrated on steadying the drip rattling along on its portable stand with one hand, while attempting to still the restless child with the other. Six-year-old Timmy, lying on the theatre trolley, was on the edge of consciousness, fretful, with arms flailing violently.

A hand touched her shoulder. 'Harriet, could you get someone to take over from you now? This is . . .'

'No, I'm sorry, but I can't,' said Harriet briefly. Intent on her task, her mind only marginally registered the fact that it was her fiancé speaking to her, and that he was accompanied by the tall, dark stranger she had bumped into. 'I'll have to stay with this child in recovery,' she explained, giving Felix an absent-minded smile, trying to make up for her sharp reply. 'The blood loss was rather excessive, and you know how a bleeding tonsillectomy can go sour on you in recovery.'

'As soon as you can, then,' said Felix, standing back out of the way as the porters swung the trolley round. 'We'll be taking coffee in the surgeons' room. Please join us there.'

'But don't leave your small charge until you are quite happy,' the dark man said. His voice had an attractive foreign inflection and somewhere at the back of her mind, recognition bells jangled. He must be Philippe Krir, the man who was the director of the hospital in Turkey. The hospital in which Felix was determined to become visiting senior surgeon.

She knew Felix thought that if he set up and started a surgical unit in a new hospital it would be a big plus on his curriculum vitae, and if Felix wanted it, then she wanted it for him too. However, in the hassle of that morning's operating list she had completely forgotten about the director's visit. Now, after Timmy's haemorrhage, there was no chance of meeting him in the coffee break as planned. Harriet couldn't see any likelihood of getting a break of any description, at least not in the foreseeable future.

'I've no intention of leaving my patient, sir,' she said, in answer to his remark. Adding politely, 'I do hope to be able to join you, but it may not be possible.'

Her gaze was caught and trapped by a pair of golden-flecked topaz eyes smiling into hers. Even though she was preoccupied with her patient, there was something about the man's face that struck her like a physical blow. He was not handsome in the conventional sense of the word. He had a compelling kind of attractiveness, fierce and yet strangely kind. The wide, sensual, yet humorous mouth invited her to smile back at him, and Harriet found that she was responding involuntarily, and to her fury felt herself blushing too.

'Please try,' said Felix. Harriet heard a note of urgency in his voice and knew he was anxious to make a good impression.

'I will.' She felt guilty because she had forgotten. Looking back over her shoulder she could see that Felix looked anything but pleased. 'I promise,' she shouted back.

The theatre porters sped along the gleaming

expanse of corridor towards the recovery area, with Harriet in tow. Once in the recovery room, Felix and his dark companion receded to the back of her mind. There were so many things to do, and not enough nurses as usual.

'Come on, let's get this child in the lateral position.'

'Oh, but I . . . oh, dear.' Student Nurse Wainwright was more of a hindrance than a help as she puffed and panted, and got more and more flustered.

Harriet kept her patience. 'Wedge a pillow in his back for support, while I hold him,' she said calmly. It was the girl's first day in the operating suite, and a massive bleed was frightening, even for staff who were used to such things.

'Yes, Sister.' The student's eyes looked enormous with worry as she scurried round to do Harriet's bidding.

'You did very well in theatre,' said Harriet. 'Most of the new girls pass out at the sight of so much blood the first time they see it.'

'Really?' Nurse Wainwright managed a wavering smile.

'Really,' affirmed Harriet.

They succeeded in settling Timmy to Harriet's satisfaction, and Nurse Wainwright transferred her worries to the drip, peering at it to make sure it wasn't blocked.

Harriet smiled reassuringly. 'What's your first name?' she asked.

'Olive,' came the breathless reply.

'Well, Olive, don't look so worried,' she said. 'We've done the most important thing, got him settled so that a good airway can be maintained.' She glanced at the plasma bag; it was dripping with slow regularity from the giving set on the stand. No problem there. She handed Olive a chart. 'Now you can monitor the vital signs for the next hour as he regains full consciousness.'

Olive ticked them off one by one on the chart. 'Temperature, pulse, respiration, blood pressure and level of consciousness.'

'The thing to look for,' Harriet explained, 'is a pulse-rate change; this will tell you there is inadequate oxygenation of the blood.'

'Oh, dear, what shall I do if it does change?' Olive's voice rose an octave in panic.

'Tell me,' said Harriet gently. 'I shall be here, I'm not going anywhere. As this was the last theatre case, I can stay in recovery with you.'

'But Mr Hamilton-Wirrell said you were to go to the surgeons' room as soon as possible,' Olive reminded her.

'Oh, damn!' In the short time they had been in recovery she had completely forgotten about Felix and his request to join him and the director of the Turkish hospital. 'He'll understand that I can't get away,' she said—mentally crossing her fingers and hoping he would!

Felix often nagged her about the way she always stayed on to supervise her patients, often way past her off duty time. But Harriet was absolutely adamant on that score—if she started a job, she always finished it. It was one of the few areas in which she and Felix really disagreed. It particularly infuriated Harriet that although he considered his own services were indispensable, he saw no reason why a nurse couldn't be relieved by another when her hours of duty were finished. Harriet always argued that it depended on the circumstances. Sometimes it was not ethical to hand over to someone else. She felt very strongly that a lack of personal commitment was demeaning to the status of nursing.

It was a full hour and a half later before she was free to leave recovery. 'Are you still going to the surgeons' room?' asked Olive in surprise.

Harriet sighed and glanced at the big wall clock in recovery. 'I'd better go as a token gesture,' she said, pulling a rueful face. She hurried back towards the surgeons' room, feeling quite shattered. Teaching Olive Wainwright had been exhausting.

'We had lunch,' said Felix, by way of explanation, seeing the surprised look on Harriet's face as she pushed open the door. 'And then came back.'

'At my insistence,' said his companion with a faint smile, his strange golden eyes fixed on her with a fiery glow.

Now that Harriet looked at him properly, she

realised that her first impression had vastly underestimated him. He was a very, very attractive man indeed. Although, personally, she preferred blonds like Felix, she knew that most women would have gone quite weak at the knees when confronted by the man who now stood leaning against the door of the surgeons' room. He was tall, with broad shoulders, his hair was black, and the strange golden topaz eyes that seemed to fluctuate with different colours were fringed by sooty dark lashes. His eyebrows, too, were black, almost straight, but with an arrogant quirk to them.

There was an explosive quality about him. He looked the kind of man who could get fearsomely angry, although at the moment he was smiling encouragingly enough. That, however, didn't stop Harriet from automatically making a mental note—mustn't upset *him*!

'I'm glad you did,' she said, and to her horror felt herself beginning to blush again.

The wretched man was making her uncomfortably aware that she was not looking her best—not something that usually bothered her when working. But now, she was painfully conscious that a morning in the paediatric theatre, with its artificially raised temperature, perfect for small unconscious patients but hell for the staff, had not enhanced her appearance one iota.

'You missed lunch again, I suppose,' said

Felix.

'Yes,' confessed Harriet, knowing it always gave her a wan look with dark shadows under her eyes.

To make matters worse, the only theatre dress available that morning from the communal cupboard had been a small size, reduced to minuscule proportions by excessive laundering. Harriet felt as if she had been poured into it, which indeed had practically been the case! Illogically she wished suddenly that her legs were shorter, so that not quite so much of them was revealed. She slipped a hand furtively behind her back, and tried, without much success, to ease the hem down a little. A loud cough from Felix caught her attention; he was glowering pointedly at her head. Oh, heavens! She still had the unbecoming theatre cap pulled tightly over her head, and Felix hated her in it. He always said she looked like 'Mrs Mop'.

Ripping off the paper cap, she shook the shining cap of her short dark hair free. 'I'm Harriet Jones,' she said formally, with as much aplomb as could be mustered in the circumstances. She held out her hand. 'You must be Dr Philippe Krir, the director of Bodrum Hospital.'

'Right first time,' he said, taking her hand between his two enormous ones. 'How are you?'

Harriet felt an inexplicable shiver run the length of her spine as his warm hands touched hers. 'Very well, thank you,' she heard herself saying in a stilted voice.

Was it her imagination, or did his eyes keep straying down to her legs? Damned dress, why couldn't the hospital keep a decent supply in the cupboard?

'I had intended to give you a formal interview,' Harriet forced herself to concentrate on what he was saying. 'But I can see this is neither the time nor the place. But as Felix has given me such a glowing report on your abilities, I am quite happy to offer you a post at Bodrum if you wish to take it.'

'Oh, yes, I do,' said Harriet quickly.

In truth she wasn't madly keen, but Felix was anxious that she should be with him, so she had promised to go.

'Why? Are you unhappy here?'

The directness of the question surprised her. She opened her mouth to say that reason was so that she could be with her fiancé, but before she could say a word Felix butted in.

'I've persuaded Harriet that she will benefit from the additional experience,' he said. 'It will stand her in good stead for promotion at a later date. And, of course, from my own point of view, it will be good to have a nursing colleague in whom I have absolute trust.'

Harriet thought he'd gone a bit over the top. Why on earth couldn't he have told the truth? she thought irritably. She wondered if Philippe

Krir was thinking it odd, because his answer was a long time in coming.

'I see.' The eventual answer was slow, and his eyes narrowed reflectively as he looked down at her. Harriet found herself blushing guiltily, and wished again that Felix had told the plain unvarnished truth. But she hastily composed her features as Philippe Krir turned towards her and said, 'Well, Miss Jones, we'll meet again in Bodrum. I look forward to it.' Then with a distinctively dismissive movement he glanced at his watch and said to Felix, 'I must leave you now. I have another appointment the other side of London.'

'Of course.' Felix beamed from ear to ear. Like the Cheshire Cat, thought Harriet. She knew that smile, it meant everything had gone as planned!

The two men left before Harriet had a chance to utter another word, leaving her standing in the corridor. Their reflections flickered on the polished floor as they walked away, disappearing abruptly as they turned the corner out of sight.

'Oh, well, in for a penny, in for a pound!' she said, voicing her thoughts out loud.

She sat down and penned her resignation there and then, before the reservations niggling at the back of her mind got the better of her. Felix would never forgive her if she backed out now!

The letter safely delivered to the nursing officer's secretary, Harriet thought about the future. In one month's time, she would be leaving London for Turkey. She hoped she and Felix were doing the right thing. Philippe Krir had seemed charming, but there was something about him which gave Harriet a peculiar feeling in the pit of her stomach. He had unsettled her. The annoying thing was that she couldn't exactly pinpoint why.

'Oh, by the way, you'd better take that off. I should have mentioned it before but I forgot.' Felix nodded his handsome head towards the sapphire and diamond engagement ring sparkling on Harriet's finger.

Harriet looked at him in surprise, at the same time thinking for the hundred and first time how similar to Robert Redford he looked. His blond hair glinted in the light of the sun streaming in through the porthole window of the aircraft, his eyes seemed bluer than ever and the line of his jaw was perfection itself, strong and determined.

She smiled lovingly. He *was* strong and determined, otherwise he could never have persuaded her to accompany him to southern Turkey, to work in a new hospital. She had been quite happy working at St James's in central London, and not particularly keen to go off to what she suspected would turn out to be fairly primitive conditions.

Twiddling the expensive engagement ring around on her finger, she looked at Felix and raised her eyebrows in query. 'Take it off? Whatever for?'

'One of Philippe Krir's little idiosyncrasies is that he only wants "unattached" people working for him. When I recommended you as a nursing sister with good experience, I naturally didn't mention that we were engaged.'

'Why naturally?' Harriet frowned. Sometimes Felix annoyed her by arranging things without consulting her. Making decisions as if she wasn't capable. 'I can't think that's a good reason to hide our engagement,' she continued. 'It's never interfered in our working relationship before, so why should it now? You should have told him.'

'Look, Harriet.' For a moment Felix sounded exasperated. 'I wouldn't have got the post of senior surgeon, with all the experience and opportunities it offers me, if he'd even got a whiff of the fact that I was engaged to be married. So for the next eighteen months we are going to be unengaged—to all intents and purposes.' His tone softened and he reached across and stroked her hand persuasively. 'Don't be cross with me, darling. I didn't want to leave you behind for over a year; after all you haven't any family, only me. I did it for your sake.'

'For your sake, you mean,' said Harriet crossly. Then just as quickly as the thought flickered through her mind, she banished it. 'Sorry, darling, that was a bit uncharitable,' she apologised.

'I really didn't feel I could mention it,' said Felix, looking slightly embarrassed. 'And I thought you agreed that this was a terrific opportunity for both of us. Not just me.' Now he sounded slightly aggrieved and Harriet felt guilty.

She sighed. 'You're probably right, but I do think it might have been worth sounding him out first.' She slipped off the engagement ring and gave it to Felix for safe keeping. 'Maybe Philippe Krir is not as strict about unattached employees as you think. He might be quite easy-going,' she added hopefully.

'You wait until you meet him properly. You've only had a brief encounter in a hospital corridor,' grinned Felix, happy now he had the ring safely in his wallet. 'Philippe Krir is a real slave-driver. I remember the first time I met him, he was in his office and something, or someone, had just annoyed him. His face was black as thunder and he was barking orders down the telephone.' He laughed, 'He might be half French, but believe me he thinks as a Turkish despot, and when he says jump he expects everyone to jump!'

'Well, here's someone who won't be doing a whole lot of jumping,' said Harriet flippantly. But she shivered just the same. Felix had put into words the intangible feeling she'd had about Philippe Krir. He was a man used to getting his own way. Instinctively she knew that he would pursue whatever he wanted, until it was within his grasp. 'Anyway, Felix,' she said lightly, 'now is a fine time to frighten me to death with a fearsome description of my new employer. I'm half-way to Turkey now and can't go back!'

'Don't worry, I'll be there to protect you,' said Felix soothingly, 'and anyway, you probably won't have too much to do with him. As he's the director, I don't suppose he'll have much time for the nurses.'

With that Felix forgot about Philippe Krir as their in-flight meal was served. He poured Harriet a generous glass of wine, and set about relaxing and enjoying the meal. Not so Harriet, however; the image of the tall dark man with the intimidating, hypnotic eyes flashed before her, and she picked at her food and worried about the future. How would she get on in a strange country with strange customs and, if Felix was to be believed, a slave-driver for a boss? She thought, with a sudden wistful longing, of her neat little London flat, with its colourful Habitat furniture, and wondered what the accommodation would be like in Turkey.

Looking around the huge Tristar aircraft, she wondered if any of the other passengers were bound for the new Bodrum Hospital. She knew other people had been interviewed in London, so surely she and Felix couldn't be the only ones going? There was one other girl, she decided, who could be a possible candidate. She was about the same age as Harriet, with hair as blonde as her own was dark.

The girl was talking animatedly to her neighbour, an elderly lady, making her laugh with whatever it was she was saying. She looked as if she would be fun to be with, and Harriet hoped she was a nurse destined for Bodrum like herself. She had a premonition that she would need a friend. Felix was always very preoccupied with his surgery at the best of times. Now he was to be the only surgeon in the hospital for a while, it would inevitably mean he'd be very busy indeed.

The flight to Dalaman in southern Turkey took nearly four hours. Harriet was disappointed to find it dark when they arrived. 'I was longing to see what the countryside looked like,' she said.

'You'll see soon enough.' Felix wasn't nearly as curious as Harriet, and only wanted to get to the hospital.

After the crowded bustle of Gatwick, the airport at Dalaman presented a very different picture. No blazing mass of lights, or satellite shuttle for the passengers. Instead, all they could see was a large, austere and very dimly lit terminal building, composed of concrete slabs, and a few huts to one side. An icy wind whistled across the tarmac and round the buildings, adding to the air of gloom.

'I thought Turkey was supposed to be hot,' muttered Harriet to Felix. She pulled her thin cardigan tightly around her and, along with the rest of the passengers, negotiated the steep steps down to the tarmac.

'Apparently they are having an unseasonably cold spell,' he replied cheerfully. He was snug, having had the foresight to pack his anorak.

Harriet glowered at him balefully, and cursed herself for ignoring his advice on packing her own anorak. He had been proved irritatingly correct! His motto was be prepared for anything, whereas Harriet always veered on the optimistic side and was inclined to take chances; now she knew she had no one but herself to blame for being cold. Usually cheerful, she felt anything but cheerful that night, especially when the stewardess informed them that they would have to collect their own luggage from the mountain of cases piled up on the tarmac beside the plane. A loud groan made her turn round. It was the blonde girl she'd noticed on the plane.

'I never thought I'd get frostbite in Turkey, and a slipped disc into the bargain!' she said. She pulled a rueful face at Harriet and began to laugh. 'This is what they call in at the deep end, I suppose,' she said as she dived into the jumbled mountain of luggage, and heaved a case from the pile.

Harriet grinned back. The mere sound of the girl's bubbly laughter was infectious. 'Where is your destination?' she asked, hoping it was the same as hers.

'Bodrum, I'm a . . .'

'Nurse?' interrupted Harriet delightedly.

'Why yes, and you? Are you going to the new hospital in Bodrum too?'

'Yes. I've travelled over with . . .' She stopped suddenly. She'd been about to blurt out 'my fiancé', and had remembered just in time that she was not engaged for the time being. 'With a surgeon who used to work at the same hospital as me,' she finished hastily.

'Oh, that gorgeous Robert Redford-looking type. I noticed him on the plane. Where is he, by the way? I do think he could give a hand to two damsels in distress.'

As she spoke, Felix suddenly materialised beside them. He had managed to retrieve both his own and Harriet's luggage.

'Hi. My name's Suzy,' said the blonde girl, who certainly didn't suffer from shyness. 'Suzy MacDonald. I understand you are both bound for the new Bodrum Hospital too.'

Harriet caught the flash of alarm that passed across his face, and knew Felix was wondering what information she had given out.

'This is Mr Felix Hamilton-Wirrell,' she said formally, 'the new surgeon for Bodrum, and I'm Harriet Jones. We travelled together, as we both used to work at St James's, London.'

'I would have got a seat with you if I'd

known,' Suzy chattered on happily. 'I can tell you, I began to wonder if I was the only one recruited to work in the place. Not that I would have been at all surprised at that! Tall, dark and handsome Mr Krir might be, but he nearly succeeded in putting me right off. Talk about a grilling; he practically barbecued me!'

She was prevented from going into greater detail as they drew near the immigration and passport control desks. It took Suzy all her powers of persuasion to explain that every jar and bottle she carried in her assorted hand luggage was essential.

'Probably suspected of drug smuggling,' observed Felix acidly. He and Harriet were in another queue opening their bags for inspection. 'Why on earth a woman has to carry that much junk I don't know.'

'Some women just do,' said Harriet, feeling defensive for her new-found friend, and women in general.

'I wouldn't allow you to,' said Felix loftily.

'You wouldn't have any say in the matter. Especially now that we're not engaged,' retorted Harriet tartly. The words popped out before she could stop them.

She saw Felix give her a startled look, and hid an inward smile as she passed ahead of him and through passport control. She usually kept her thoughts to herself, so Felix wasn't used to sharp comments. But suddenly she felt defiant, and without his ring on her finger she also felt uncannily free. The next eighteen months are going to do us both good, she thought with a sudden flash of insight.

Once outside the airport building, they were joined by Suzy. 'A coach was supposed to meet us here, and take us on to Bodrum,' said Felix looking around.

There was no coach for them. Most of the other people were holidaymakers, and boarded gleaming air-conditioned coaches with various destinations marked on the front in English and Turkish. There was one for Bodrum, but that was completely full of tourists. One by one the buses departed, until they were the only people standing in the freezing cold night, except for one other person. A tall, very thin and tanned young man.

He wandered across to them. 'Good day, or rather should I say goodnight,' he said in a broad Australian accent. 'You wouldn't be waiting for the coach to Bodrum Hospital, would you?'

'We are,' said Felix grimly. The cold had begun to penetrate even his anorak, and he wasn't looking quite so cheerful.

The Australian looked at Suzy and Harriet. They were now standing huddled together for warmth, and had long since resigned themselves to ending up with frostbite. 'Nurses?' he queried.

They both nodded. 'And due for a spell in

intensive care if we don't get in somewhere warm soon,' Harriet said through chattering teeth.

'Barry South, paediatric physician extraordinaire,' said the Australian, bending down and unzipping a compartment on his shabby haversack, the only luggage he had with him. From the pocket he drew out a large bottle of Metaxa brandy. 'Picked this up cheap in Greece,' he said with a grin. 'It'll probably rot your guts, but at least it will warm you up in the meantime.'

He passed the bottle around, and there was silence as they all, took a grateful swig of the fiery liquid. Although it was rough, it was also warming, and Harriet looked around her, feeling more cheerful.

'You don't think . . .' she began, pointing towards a corner of the car park where a dusty minibus was parked. The word Bodrum was marked on the front in faded letters, and they could just make out the slumped form of a man, apparently sound asleep in the front seat.

'Yep. I do,' replied the Australian, and started purposefully towards the parked vehicle.

'I'm afraid he's right,' said Felix, looking anything but pleased. 'I had expected better transport than this, but I suppose anything that gets us to our destination is better than nothing.'

'Do you really think that's it?' Suzy was dubious.

'Definitely!' said Harriet. 'Come on.'

The girls followed Felix, dragging their luggage across the dusty car park. By now it was midnight, and they were all beginning to feel distinctly frayed at the edges.

Once Barry had aroused the sleeping driver, it did indeed turn out to be the transport hired to take them to Bodrum. The driver was profuse in his apologies, and gave them a long, rambling explanation, accompanied by much hand-waving, and flashing of white teeth. But as his English was limited, and their Turkish non-existent, they could only guess at half of what he was saying.

'At least we know the natives are friendly,' whispered Suzy as the teeth flashed expansively once more.

Harriet giggled, and subdued a hiccup. The brandy must have been stronger than she thought!

'I shall have a word with Krir about this,' said Felix, shooting Harriet a disapproving glance. It was unlike her to be giggly! 'This really isn't good enough.' His last words catapulted out as the driver revved the engine like mad, and the bus started off with a flying leap into space.

'Hell, you can't expect him to waste money on fancy transport when he needs every penny for the hospital project,' said Barry, passing the brandy bottle around again. 'I've hitch-hiked from Australia to Turkey,' he said, stretching out his long legs, 'and believe me, this is luxury compared to some of my modes of travel. Did seventy miles on a camel once, couldn't walk for a week afterwards!'

'Gosh,' said Suzy admiringly. 'I wish I could do something exciting like that.'

'Me too,' said Harriet.

'This is quite exciting enough for me,' grumbled Felix, taking the thickest blanket from the pile on the floor. He wrapped himself in it with an ill grace. 'It's not good enough,' he repeated, before turning over and falling asleep.

Wrapping themselves in blankets like cocoons, Barry and the girls tried to settle for a few hours' sleep.

'Good-looking, but a bit of a stuffed shirt, that Felix chap,' whispered Suzy in Harriet's ear, 'but I suppose he can't help it. He *is* a surgeon, after all!'

'Yes,' to her surprise, Harriet found herself agreeing.

It was the first time she'd ever seen Felix in a situation where he was not in complete control. He obviously didn't like roughing it, although he must have had some idea of what it would be like; he usually investigated everything thoroughly. Sleepily she tried to remember what little Felix had told her about Turkey, but the strong brandy and exhaustion took their toll. Like the others, she fell asleep.

The sliding door of the minibus was thrown

back with resounding vigour, awakening the occupants with a jolt. Harriet, sitting nearest the door, looked up into the formidable face she remembered with surprising clarity. A face the colour of burnished copper. Later, she thought it must have been because she was half asleep that it seemed the speculative amber eyes looked at her for a moment with something akin to tenderness. But it was only a fleeting moment, and in a second the look had gone, to be replaced with a courteous but distinctly remote expression.

His ringing tone of voice dispelled any remnants of sleep. 'Good morning, everyone. I have arranged breakfast for you here.'

He waved an imperious hand in the direction of a long, two-storey whitewashed building. They were in a small square, surrounded by white houses, huddling cheek by jowl with one another. Purple bougainvillaea ran riot, up the walls and along the flat roofs, providing a vivid splash of colour.

'Great,' said Suzy, jumping out first. 'I say,' she whispered to Harriet, 'do you think this is the hospital?'

'It's pretty small . . .' began Harriet.

'This is a hotel.' Philippe Krir had overheard their conversation. 'After breakfast, you will be taken to your quarters up at the hospital.'

'I thought we'd go straight to the hospital and have breakfast there.' Felix still sounded cross as he followed Suzy and Harriet.

'Oh, didn't you know?' Suzy stopped following Philippe for a moment, and grinned wickedly at Felix. 'The hospital is self-catering, for patients *and* staff. Your cushy days at St James's are well and truly over.'

Harriet suppressed an urge to giggle again as Felix snorted with annoyance. It was well known throughout the medical world that at St James's they had stuck to the old traditions.

'I always used to envy you the luxury of the doctors' mess,' she said. 'As a mere nurse, I either had to go home and get my own, or queue up in the canteen for the staple fare of egg and chips.'

'I can see we'll have to get a rota going for you girls to do the cooking,' said Felix, ignoring Harriet's comment.

'Forget it,' said Suzy firmly. 'Emancipated women like us don't wait hand and foot on mere men. Do we?' She looked at Harriet for confirmation.

'Certainly not,' said Harriet equally firmly, adding mischievously, 'Why, I hardly know you, Felix. Why should I cook for you? Whatever next!'

Both girls hung back, laughing at Felix's outraged expression as he stalked on ahead. It was only Harriet, however, who had an idea of the true reason. Whenever they ate together, she had always done the cooking; Felix had expected it and she had tended to acquiesce rather than continually argue. But now it was going to be different, and again she felt a *frisson* of wicked delight at her newly acquired freedom, and grinned back at Suzy.

'We don't really have to do our catering,' whispered Suzy, giving an outsize wink, 'but it won't hurt him to think it's true for a while.'

Harriet laughed. 'Amen to that!' she said.

'I hope this isn't going to be a habit. Nurses giggling and dawdling like schoolchildren.' The acid tones of their new employer interrupted their laughter.

'I was not aware that we were giggling or dawdling, and I resent your reference to schoolchildren,' retorted Harriet without stopping to think. 'After the long and uncomfortable journey we've had, you should be grateful that we have any sense of humour left at all!'

She swept past him, head held high, sleek dark hair blowing in the breeze that had sprung up from the Bodrum harbour, anger giving her lithe step a spring. Although she'd always shown Felix deference because she loved him, she had never been a doormat. She was a professional woman, and expected to be treated as such. Philippe Krir's remark had succeeded in making her hackles rise. Perhaps he thinks women are lower down in the pecking order of life, she concluded crossly. If so, then there was one Turkish doctor in Bodrum who was in for a few surprises. And Harriet knew she would be very happy to deliver them!

Suzy scuttled after her. But not before she'd noticed a look of grudging admiration flicker across the dark face of Philippe Krir. I must tell Harriet, she thought, that he likes spirited women! But, being Suzy, she promptly forgot all about it.

CHAPTER TWO

'THIS is a bit peculiar,' hissed Suzy, eyeing the breakfast laid before them.

'It's certainly different,' agreed Barry.

On the table were plates piled high with hard-boiled eggs, cold sausages and olives. The only thing that looked familiar was the freshly baked bread, pots of yoghurt and dark treacly honey.

Harriet tried the tea. 'It's very refreshing,' she said, sipping from the tiny glass cup.

'The hotel manager has tried to give you an English breakfast.' Philippe Krir gave a wry smile as he joined them. He perched on the edge of a chair, stretching his long legs before him. Harriet, still shivering from the cold, was envious of the thick fisherman-type sweater, and warm corded trousers with knee-high leather boots he was wearing.

An uneasy silence reigned for a few seconds. Then Harriet suddenly noticed the manager standing behind Philippe. His chubby brown face was creased with worry, and he was smoothing his spotless white apron nervously.

'It's very kind of him to go to so much trouble,' she said quickly, and, spearing a hard-boiled egg, ate it with apparent relish. 'Delicious,' she pronounced firmly.

After a moment's hesitation, the others followed suit, and the manager, reassured at last that he had pleased his guests, disappeared back into the kitchen, a happy smile of contentment wreathing his face.

Philippe leaned across the table towards Harriet. 'Kindness and tact will go far with the Turkish people,' he said approvingly, adding with an amused smile, 'but you needn't eat *all* the hard-boiled eggs just to prove how delicious they are!'

His eyes were fixed on her with an intensity she found unnerving, and, just as she had when she had first met him in the operating theatre suite, Harriet felt a hot colour flooding her face.

'The poor man looked so worried,' she muttered hurriedly, tearing her gaze away from the tawny eyes threatening to mesmerise her.

She let her long dark lashes flutter down, effectively masking her expressive green eyes, and tried to concentrate on the breakfast before her.

Suzy provided a welcome interruption. 'What shall we call you?' she asked. 'Dr Krir? Mr Krir? The director, or what?'

'Ah, you English. Why do you always want to know exactly where you stand?' He gave a velvet chuckle, and Harriet thought how warm and how very masculine he sounded. 'You must call me Philippe, of course, and I shall call all of you by your first names. Now, let me see.' He looked at Suzy. 'It's Suzy, isn't it?' Then he looked at Harriet. 'And you are Harriet Jones, the colleague of Felix next to you.'

He spoke as if he was trying to remember, but as she looked at him Harriet saw that he remembered everything, including her tendency to blush. He was not the type to forget details! He turned his attention to Barry South. 'As there are only two men, and I know Felix, you must be the Australian paediatrician recommended to me, Barry South.'

Introductions finished, he left them to get on with their breakfast, after informing them that their driver, Ali, the one who'd driven them from Dalaman, would bring them up to the hospital when they were ready. His smile encompassed the whole table as he spoke. And although she knew it was irrational, it still seemed to Harriet that there was a sudden lick of fire in the depths of his eyes as his gaze lingered momentarily on her. She looked away quickly, before he could see she was blushing again.

An hour later they piled back into the minibus, and set off for the hospital. Refreshed and wide awake now, they looked around them with curiosity as the bus chugged off erratically. The route took them through the main square of Bodrum, past the mosque and a colourful market selling everything from goats to spices. The scene looked idyllic in the early-morning light, but suddenly the air was rent asunder by an ear-splitting voice, rising and falling in wailing cadences. They looked at one another in astonishment.

Their driver Ali grinned as he saw their faces in his driving mirror. 'Muezzin calling,' he said, pointing at the pearly white minaret of the mosque they were passing.

'Is the hospital far from the mosque?' asked Barry hopefully.

'Yes, is far, but you hear muezzin,' said Ali cheerfully. Taking his hands off the wheel, he explained in mime how this miracle was achieved.

'Oh, my God!' moaned Suzy, covering her eyes, as the unfettered bus nearly ran over two goats and several market stall holders.

'Aah, I get it,' Barry nodded vigorously and hastily directed an unperturbed Ali's attention back to the steering wheel. 'We can hear muezzin everywhere.'

'Everywhere,' said Ali, flashing his white teeth again.

'I think they call five times a day,' said Harriet, letting her breath out slowly, relieved when Ali's eyes were fixed once more on the road.

Suzy nodded. 'One more hour before sunrise, three times in the day, and the last, one hour after sunset.' She read this information from the guide book she'd fished out of her pocket.

'No need to set the alarm, then,' said Barry grinning.

'I think it sounds lovely,' said Harriet, 'so . . .'

'Foreign,' interrupted Felix sarcastically, 'but one can hardly put it in the lovely category!'

'I agree with Harriet,' piped up Suzy. 'It sounds lovely. It makes me feel that I've really embarked on an exciting adventure and that anything might happen. And as for Philippe Krir, he's gorgeous; he can sweep me up on to his horse and carry me off to his tent any day!' She gave an exaggerated sigh.

Harriet laughed. 'He drove off in a jeep,' she said, 'not the most romantic of chariots. And anyway, I thought you didn't like him at your interview.'

'That was then, this is now,' said Suzy mysteriously, as if that was a rational explanation for everything.

Harriet said nothing, although she could easily understand Suzy's growing fascination with Philippe. There was something very vibrant and compelling about his bronzed face—indeed, about his whole person. He oozed an almost primitive, raw masculinity. He definitely wasn't a man one could forget in a hurry. It had surprised her to find how clearly he had remained in her own mind after just one encounter. Feeling a twinge of guilt at such thoughts, she glanced across at Felix and gave him a secret smile. To her delight he smiled back. The first real smile he'd given her since they had arrived in Turkey.

Suddenly she felt happier. They'd be able to slip off together sometimes. Felix would be able to arrange that, she was sure. He was so good at arranging things.

By now the minibus had climbed the steep hills encircling Bodrum. Looking down, Harriet could see the whole town nestling into the hillside. White houses, hung with vivid purple and red bougainvillaea, rose tier upon tier against the green hills overlooking the blue waters of the bay. The bay itself was guarded by a great medieval castle, its massive stone walls jutting out into the sea.

'The castle of St Peter, built by the Crusader Knights of Rhodes,' said Suzy, sounding like a tour courier, as she consulted the guide book again.

'Yes, and built with stones plundered from the Mausoleum of Halicarnassus, once one of the seven wonders of the ancient world,' said Barry reading over her shoulder and mimicking her accent. 'Fancy that, the Brits were vandals even in those days!'

'I imagine a fortress to guard the harbour was considered by the British to be more important than a mere tomb,' said Felix in what could only be described as his British Raj voice!

'God, you sound pompous,' said Suzy tactlessly.

'Well, I . . . really!' Felix stuttered into outraged silence.

Harriet wanted to laugh but thought better of it. Instead she said, 'I wonder when we're going to get there.'

But no sooner had she spoken than the minibus rounded a corner and they were confronted by an enormous building, perched on a promontory of land which jutted out of the mountainside. At the top of the building, rows of ornate arches looked out towards the bay of Bodrum, but below, the white stone walls were blank and windowless except for a few small slits. At ground level, in the middle of the huge expanse of blank wall, was an enormous gateway, set in an elaborately carved archway. Ali drove the bus through the gateway into a paved courtyard.

The sun chose this particular moment to break through the thinning cloud, and the whiteness of the stones beneath their feet was dazzling. The whole courtyard was a blaze of light.

'But this isn't a hospital. It's a palace of some sort,' said Felix, staring around with disbelief.

'It *was* a palace, and is now a hospital.' Philippe suddenly appeared, materialising from within the depths of the monumental building. ' "The Palace of Love Divine", built by a sultan in the fourteenth century, and so called because legend has it that he had an insatiable appetite for women.'

Harriet stared at him. It wasn't her imagination, there was definitely an undertone of mocking sensuality in his voice.

It reeked of chauvinism and annoyed her. 'How interesting,' she said icily. 'The sultan would have quite a shock if he came back now. Finding the place full of sick patients, looked after and organised by emancipated western women.'

He twisted his lips into a wry smile. 'I wonder how emancipated you really are,' he said.

'Very,' said Suzy firmly, 'when it comes to work.'

'I shall remember that,' teased Barry, 'when you've got a headache.'

Harriet sensed that Barry had butted in because he could feel the hostility emanating from herself and Suzy. She stared back at Philippe, determined not to drop her eyes first.

'Where are the wards and theatres?' asked Felix, looking around.

Harriet and Suzy looked at each other, and Suzy raised her eyebrows. They were both glad the subject had got back on to the familiar territory of hospital matters. Although Harriet doubted that Felix had any inkling of how either of them felt. He could be pretty chauvinistic himself.

Philippe waved his right hand. 'This half of the palace has been converted into the hospital. We have two adult surgical, two paediatric—surgical and medical—and two adult medical wards. Two theatres, one adult and one paediatric, and a recovery room.'

'What about intensive care, and a reception area for casualties?' Harriet asked.

Out of the corner of her eye she saw Felix frown, and knew he was thinking she should have left the questioning to him. She felt annoyed again. What was the matter with her? She didn't usually feel so aggressively feminist!

'Those too,' answered Philippe, 'and drugs, and some but not all equipment. Does that satisfy you, Miss Jones?' Suddenly without warning he flashed her a smile.

'Yes, thank you,' said Harriet primly, determined not to smile back. He needn't think that because he decided to turn on the charm she would succumb!

Felix attracted his attention, and Harriet studied her new boss as he prowled about the courtyard while answering the questions Felix fired at him. He blended in perfectly with the surroundings, and Harriet found herself imagining how he would look with a burnous wrapped around him. His face half hidden by an Arab head-dress, instead of the western clothes he was wearing. It was a strangely disturbing picture, and she shivered violently.

'You are cold.' Immediately Philippe was at her side. He looked down at Harriet with concern, and then at Suzy. 'Both of you are not properly dressed for this weather,' he said in a voice that held a hint of reprimand. 'I cannot have my English nurses becoming ill before they have even done any work.'

'According to my book——' Suzy waved her ever-present guide book under his nose '—it says that the temperature in late spring is usually twenty-one degrees Celsius. So I came prepared for sunshine.'

'So did I,' murmured Harriet.

'Never believe everything you read in books,' was the abrupt answer. Then, swinging on his heel, he spoke to Ali in rapid Turkish before turning back to the small group. 'Ali will take the men to their quarters,' he said, indicating some archways on the left-hand side of the courtyard. 'I will take the girls to theirs.' He picked up most of their luggage. 'You bring the rest and——'

A loud clanging, echoing cavernously from the depths of the palace, interrupted him. Philippe dropped the luggage and started to run. 'Something is wrong in the casualty-room,' he said. With one accord they followed him. 'The internal phones will be installed next week,' he shouted over his shoulder. 'Until then we have bells.'

The deep continuous clanging reverberated in their eardrums. 'Much more dramatic than a phone call,' said Harriet.

'I'll say,' Suzy puffed.

They entered the large casualty area close on

the heels of Philippe. A youth of about eighteen years lay on the trolley. He was in shock, sweating profusely and his breathing laboured. A great patch of dark, stale blood stained the front of his shirt.

'A knife wound to the chest, Doctor.' A dark girl in the uniform of an auxiliary was by the patient. 'He seemed to be all right, and I thought he could wait until you came, but——'

'Don't worry, Laila,' Philippe said calmly, 'you've done the right thing. Have you X-rayed yet?'

She nodded and passed him an X-ray. Philippe slotted it into the wall-mounted screen and the three men crowded round to look.

Without waiting for instructions, Harriet and Suzy moved across to the patient and began stripping off his shirt. 'The jugular vein is raised,' called Harriet. 'It looks as if the pericardium has been penetrated.'

Suzy took the blood pressure. 'Pressure's dropping fast,' she said, 'OK, Laila, let's get an ECG on him.' She smiled at the young Turkish girl, by now grey with worry.

'Don't worry too much,' said Harriet, knowing the poor girl was probably blaming herself. 'This type of patient can go downhill very quickly.' She forced herself to smile too, and hoped the girl understood. But both she and Suzy knew that if indeed the pericardium has been penetrated, it meant that the sac which protected the heart was filled with blood. Then the blood would build up in pressure against the heart, preventing it from beating properly.

As if in answer to her thoughts she heard Felix say, 'Pericardial tamponade. The heart has a hole in it and the lung is collapsed.'

'Let's get a tube in and expand the lung.' Philippe's voice was very quiet, but there was no mistaking the urgency. 'We're going to anaesthetise and open him up.'

Thankful that a properly laid-up trolley was already there, Harriet passed an endotracheal tube to Philippe. As soon as the tube was in position, she began to squeeze the bag in a steady rhythm. Philippe flashed her an approving glance, but Harriet was too busy to notice. All eyes were fixed on the ECG monitor. Although the lungs were ventilating, the monitor was slowing, then the curve went flat, into the straight line that spelled death.

'He's gone—damn.' Barry's voice was soft.

'A thoracotomy. We've got nothing to lose—scalpel.' At times like this, Felix was a superb doctor. His highly trained surgeon's brain worked at lightning speed.

Philippe handed him the scalpel. 'Go ahead.'

Felix slashed the sharp blade across the patient's chest. Hardly any blood spurted, an ominous sign as they all knew. It meant the heart was trapped in the pericardium.

'Retractor.' Again Philippe passed it to Felix.

The retractor inserted, Felix pulled and spread the ribs open with one swift movement. Still the ECG monitor was straight, a monotonous moan instead of a bleep filling the room.

'Scissors. Now stand back.'

Felix bent over to reach the pericardial sac, and snipped the scissors into it. A jet of blood shot out under pressure from the heart sac, splattering everyone. No one spoke. All eyes were on the monitor as Felix began to massage the heart.

The monitor gave a small bleep, then was silent.

'Hell, no go,' muttered Barry.

But suddenly the bleep sounded again, and again, and then a regular rhythm was established.

Harriet felt for the pulse. 'It's just palpable,' she reported.

'We haven't won the battle yet,' said Philippe, 'let's get him into theatre.'

Within minutes the patient was on the operating table, and Harriet and Suzy were ripping open a box of plasma expander and setting up a drip.

'Transfuse a thousand cc's,' said Philippe. 'We'll have to manage with Gelofusin, we don't have the luxury of fresh blood.'

'We'll manage. A thirty-two chest tube please.' Felix began to repair the damage.

An hour later, the patient was safely closed

and it was smiles all round.

'A good, strong and steady heartbeat,' said Philippe with satisfaction. 'Congratulations everyone, and my apologies for the rather traumatic introduction to the Palace Hospital.'

'A case of "in at the deep end",' said Barry with a grin. 'Well, Philippe, at least you know now that we can all swim!'

Philippe laughed and the tension dissipated. 'I certainly do. Now, if you fellows don't mind staying and keeping an eye on him,' he nodded at the peacefully sleeping patient, 'I'll take the girls to their quarters.'

Felix and Barry nodded their agreement, and Philippe turned away. 'Come on,' he said, walking ahead with long strides.

Without waiting to see if they followed, he returned to the main courtyard and picked up the luggage that had been dumped when the emergency bell had sounded. He strode in front, leaving Suzy and Harriet almost having to run to keep up with him as he led the way upstairs and down seemingly endless corridors. As they followed his tall figure, they could see passages leading off the main corridor right and left, and now and then a room with the door open gave them a glimpse of ornamental tiling, and elaborate mosaic motifs.

'This part of the building really does seem like a palace,' whispered Suzy, 'not at all like a hospital.'

Harriet agreed. 'Perfect condition, considering it has been standing for nearly four hundred years,' she commented.

Philippe paused at last, and waited for them to catch up. 'Fatima has spent a lot of money on this place,' he said.

'Fatima?' asked Harriet. Without warning a spasm of alarm shot through her. Perhaps he was married and Fatima was his wife.

Suzy with her usual irrepressible curiosity provided the answer. 'Is Fatima your wife?'

Philippe appeared unperturbed by the directness of the question, and laughed. 'No, I am not married yet,' he said. 'Fatima is my benefactress. She is a rich widow, who wishes to do good for the town, and preserve this ancient palace.'

'And wishes to do a bit of good for herself if she's got any sense,' muttered Suzy under her breath from behind Harriet's back. 'I wonder how old she is.'

'Perhaps she's very old,' Harriet whispered back, knowing she was being totally irrational. It was none of her business, and she wasn't interested in Philippe anyway, she was engaged to Felix! But none the less the feeling persisted, and she mentally crossed her fingers, and hoped Fatima was old as the hills!

'If she's not old, then she just *has* to be after him,' said Suzy positively. 'Otherwise why should she agree to let this palace be turned into a hospital?'

'You're probably right,' murmured Harriet.

'I know I am,' said Suzy positively.

Contemplation of Philippe's relationship with his benefactress came to an abrupt halt, however, as she and Suzy nearly knocked him over. He had stopped without warning at a heavy wooden gate on the left of the passage, and they cannoned into him in quick succession. The panels of the gate were like little windows, each one inset with intricate brass lattice-work.

'In here,' he said.

Both girls let out a gasp of amazement as they stepped through the gateway. Before them lay a huge courtyard, this time not of dry, sunbaked stones, but paved in delicately coloured mosaics of blues and greens, shadows in the leafy forest of the fluted arches surrounding the courtyard. Behind the arches were doors. Each door was heavily decorated with gem stones. The colours glinted and winked in magnificent opulence, giving an incandescence to the dappled shadows beneath the arches.

Philippe noticed their round-eyed amazement. 'Don't worry,' he said wryly, 'the real jewels were stolen years ago, during one of the many wars that raged over the country. Those are only imitation.'

'Phew! Thank goodness for that. I should have been afraid to sleep at night,' said Suzy.

Harriet was still speechless as she looked

around, trying to take everything in. Most beautiful of all was the centre of the courtyard. Here was a large pool, hexagonal in shape, with another smaller matching hexagon in the centre. The water in the outer pool was a clear turquoise, but the small one in the centre held golden carp, and a profusion of white lilies with startlingly yellow stamens grew around the edge. Two curved bridges ran at angles into the centre, where a gazebo was swathed in rampant greenery. Harriet longed to sit on the ancient stone seat in the gazebo and admire the garden. The whole place was an education to the senses, doves cooing in the distance, a fountain bubbling in a corner, and the waters of the pool whispering languidly among the lily leaves.

'This is the most beautiful place I've ever seen,' breathed Suzy, echoing Harriet's thoughts. 'Are we really staying here?'

'Yes, all the women will stay here. This was the seraglio. A beautiful place built to please beautiful women.' He saw Suzy's puzzled expression. 'The harem,' he said with the merest inkling of a wicked smile. 'I thought it appropriate to put the girls here. You will be joined later by some more Turkish nurses I've recruited, the girls you are to train, and later another English nurse will come.'

Harriet raised her eyebrows at the word seraglio. Unlike Suzy, she knew very well what it meant. 'I take it we will be free to come and go as we please—unlike the original occupants!' she remarked drily.

The infuriating little smile he had given when he'd said it was appropriate they should stay there had raised her feminist hackles once more. That, and the fact that she realised she was desperately battling to firmly douse the undercurrent of attraction he held for her.

Philippe frowned. 'Of course. Turkey is a modern country. What did you think? That I'd lock the door?'

'I was thinking it is rather a long way from everything else,' said Harriet coolly. 'We seemed to walk for miles. Where are the men staying?'

'Why do you ask?' She knew he was annoyed as his brows lowered, and the amber colour of his eyes suddenly darkened into deep brown. 'Is it so important to be near the men? You will be quite safe here. Or perhaps you wanted to be near them for other reasons!' The sarcasm in his tone matched hers.

'Certainly not,' snapped Harriet quickly.

'I think it's lovely,' said Suzy, oblivious of the charged atmosphere between Philippe and Harriet. 'I can't wait to see my room. I shall lie in bed pretending I'm waiting for the Sultan to call on me to bestow his favours!'

Philippe didn't answer; he was checking the time, obviously anxious to get away. 'This way,' he said abruptly.

Walking towards the back of the courtyard, past the tinkling fountain, Philippe showed Suzy into her room. Harriet could hear Suzy darting about, oohing and aahing in rapture at the sumptuous fittings, while she followed Philippe's beckoning finger.

'You are four rooms away from Suzy,' he said. 'The rooms between you will be occupied by the other English girl arriving later this month, and three Turkish girls. I wanted to mix you up as much as possible. That is, if you do not object to *that*!'

'Of course not.' Harriet still felt on the defensive.

She followed him into the room and, dumping the bag she was carrying in the middle of the floor, crossed over to the windows and looked out. They were both barred. From one she could just see the minaret of the mosque in the centre of Bodrum glittering in the sun, and behind it the wide blue sweep of the bay. From the other she looked across a ravine on to the side of a mountain. Long-haired goats were grazing peacefully on the scrubby bushes and grass, and soft clanking from the bells on their necks filled the room.

'Sorry about the bars at the window, but——'

'I know, I know, this *was* the seraglio,' said Harriet irritably.

Everything about the place reminded her that

she was a woman, and that women had been dominated by men for centuries. Her feminism took another upward turn. She didn't want to be dominated, least of all by the man who was standing behind her.

Impulsively she turned to Philippe. 'Speaking as a western woman, I might as well tell you here and now that I am not happy to stay in a place which was once a prison for unhappy women.'

For a moment there was silence. Then Philippe threw back his head and roared with laughter. Harriet gritted her teeth and wished throttling someone was legal.

'I don't think the women who lived here would have agreed with you,' he said finally, between gasps of laughter. 'They lived pampered lives of luxury. Every whim catered for.'

'Every whim except one,' said Harriet fiercely. Turning away she looked out of the barred window. 'Freedom,' she said loudly. 'That whim was never theirs.'

'And are you free? Completely free?' His voice was suddenly quiet.

'Of course, I . . .'

Harriet stopped, and turned back into the room found that Philippe had moved behind her and was towering above her. His dark face looked down at her, with a penetrating gaze that seemed to probe at her very soul, digging deep at her innermost secrets.

'Yes, I am free. Free to choose the man I want. Not like the women who lived here. They had to wait here in this beautiful prison, until the Sultan chose to come to them.'

'I think it is better for a woman to wait for a man. Better a man does the chasing. I don't approve of some of this twentieth-century feminist nonsense,' he said softly. Running his forefinger slowly down her cheek, he slid his hand round the nape of her neck into her sleek dark hair. 'Who knows, Harriet, if you wait here long enough, the right man might come, even to you!'

Harriet gasped in outraged indignation, and without thinking her hand flew up and slapped the bronzed face towering above her own. But if her reflex was quick, his was even quicker. His hand snaked up and caught hers, imprisoning it before she had time to withdraw it.

'I am beginning to think, Miss Jones,' he said curtly, 'that if I had interviewed you more thoroughly, instead of taking Felix Hamilton-Wirrell's word on it, I might not have employed you.'

'And I am beginning to think that if you had interviewed me, then I *definitely* would not have come!' Harriet retorted sharply.

'Ah, but you have signed a contract now. For eighteen months!' There was a note of triumph in his voice.

'And I shall honour it,' said Harriet furiously. She wished he wasn't so close, then she could breathe more easily.

'Cooeee!' Suzy's cheerful voice echoed, bouncing off the mosaic tiles of the courtyard. 'Harriet, where are you?'

'Here,' called Harriet, wrenching her hand from Philippe's grasp, grateful for the interruption as Suzy breezed into the room.

'Lunch will be at two o'clock, make your way back to the main courtyard then,' said Philippe as he left the room.

'You've got two views,' said Suzy enviously, zooming over to the windows. 'I've only got the goats!'

Harriet threw herself on to the kingsize bed. The argument with Philippe had left her weak and trembly. She felt exhausted. 'I'm going to sleep until lunchtime,' she said, pulling the rose-coloured silk bedspread up beneath her chin.

'I rather fancied exploring,' began Suzy.

'You explore, I'll sleep,' said Harriet firmly, 'and shut the door on your way out.'

She heard the door click and almost immediately fell asleep. Her last coherent thought was of Philippe. His hawklike face was gazing down at her with the gentlest of smiles curving his lips. He should be frowning, she thought sleepily, not smiling at me like that!

CHAPTER THREE

'TWO weeks gone,' grumbled Barry, 'and we still haven't managed to get down into Bodrum to look round.' He stretched out his long thin legs which seemed to go on for ever.

It was eight o'clock in the evening, and the hospital staff had gathered together for dinner in the room converted into a dining-room. It had once been part of the Sultan's own private quarters, and the ceiling was still vivid with traditional symmetric mosaic patterns, real gold leaf shining out in parts. They were drinking the strong red wine of the district while waiting for the cook to finish his preparations.

Harriet gazed into the depths of her wine. 'Two whole weeks,' she mused.

'I feel as if I've been here for years,' said Suzy.

'Me too,' agreed Barry. 'I must say I've enjoyed the time so far, especially as Philippe has let us get on with the work in peace.'

'Yes, thank heavens,' agreed Harriet. She let her mind dwell for a moment on their new boss, and thanked her lucky stars she hadn't seen too much of him. She had only done one clinic with Philippe and had found it nerve-racking. When she and Barry worked together, as they did most of the time, she never noticed their physical closeness; he was just a pleasant colleague. But with Philippe it had been a different story. Whenever he had brushed against her, she'd felt every nerve-end in her body tighten to screaming pitch, and her heart had lurched about in her chest like a thing possessed. She was physically attracted, and yet at the same time didn't like him! An annoying combination, she thought crossly, and concentrated on the conversation washing around her.

Suzy was giggling at Barry's legs. In the two weeks they had been in Turkey, the weather had become very hot, and he was wearing shorts. 'When we go down into town, for goodness' sake don't wear those shorts,' she said. 'I've never seen such thin legs. If I didn't know the amount you eat, I'd say you were anorexic!'

Barry grinned good-naturedly. 'At least they keep the kids amused,' he said.

He and Harriet had been assigned by Philippe to run a vaccination and immunisation clinic for the local children, as protection against all the unusual childhood diseases. The hospital minibus, driven by the ever-smiling Ali, ferried children up from the town all day, every day. Harriet was happy to work in the clinic; she loved children and approved of Philippe's aim to immunise every child he could get his hands on. Her days were full, and she knew they were achieving something worthwhile.

Taking a sip of her wine, she looked across at Felix. How handsome he looked this evening in his crisp white shirt, and khaki shorts. Even the short exposure to the sun had bleached his hair even blonder, and his tanned skin showed his blue eyes to advantage. So, why isn't my heart leaping? she puzzled. But the troublesome heart in question remained mutinously still.

Idly, she listened to Felix complaining. 'It's no laughing matter,' he said to Barry. 'People like that shouldn't be let loose in intensive care.'

'Which people?' asked Harriet.

'Cleaners who unplug ventilators to plug in their hoovers.'

'What?' Philippe's voice made them all jump.

'Oh, don't worry,' said Suzy hastily, 'luckily there were no patients in the unit, and I think we made them understand that they mustn't do it again.'

'All the same, I'll speak to them,' said Philippe still frowning.

Harriet watched him as he discussed the problem with Felix. She couldn't dispel the nagging feeling that Philippe had split her and Felix up on purpose. It was strange that he should have put Suzy with Felix; she wasn't as experienced in theatre work as Harriet. Perhaps he suspected there was something more to their relationship, other than the fact that they came from the same hospital.

On the one occasion she had managed to speak to Felix alone, she had voiced her fears, and he'd agreed.

'I think we'd better be careful,' he'd said. 'I'm trying to persuade Philippe to buy a more modern operating table, and I don't want to upset him before I've had a chance to talk to his friend Fatima Mascari. He's set up a meeting with her next week to discuss the purchase.'

After that, Felix had gone out of his way never to be alone with her, and now Harriet had learned not to be hurt by his offhand treatment of her. She told herself that it was only natural for his career to come first, and it was important for him to get on well with Philippe. But she missed his company, and her life wasn't made any easier by Suzy repeating gleefully every little thing that Felix said.

That very evening, before dinner, she had confided to Harriet that she didn't think Felix would last out the eighteen months in Turkey.

'Why ever not?' Harriet's tone had been disbelieving. 'He signed a contract like the rest of us.'

'Contracts can be broken, so Felix says,' Suzy informed her airily. 'He says Philippe hasn't kept his side of the bargain, and given him all the equipment he needs.'

'This is a third world country as far as medicine is concerned,' said Harriet, feeling irritable. 'What does he expect?'

'More than he's getting,' said Suzy matter-of-factly, adding shrewdly, 'Felix is very ambitious. He came here because he thought he'd do more operating, get more cutting experience, as he puts it.'

'Yes, I'm sure he did,' said Harriet, knowing that had indeed been his motive. 'I suppose he must be a little disappointed not to be going full blast yet. But even when the theatres are fully operational, surely he realises that it will be very basic stuff? There isn't the need for sophisticated surgery.'

She wondered what he would expect her to do if he did decide to pull out and go back to England. She was enjoying her work in Turkey, and even if she didn't, she would still have felt honour bound to stay. A contract was a contract.

A niggling little worry lurked at the back of her mind. Would he ditch their engagement too, if that proved an obstacle to his advancement? And would you mind? her irritating little inner voice needled her again, but almost immediately she pushed the unwelcome thought from her mind. What was the matter with her? Felix would never be disloyal to her, and she shouldn't think disloyal thoughts. After all, he'd arranged it so that she could come all this way to be with him. It wasn't his fault that Philippe Krir had successfully separated them!

Her moody contemplation was interrupted by the arrival of the evening meal. First *mezes*, cold broad beans, stuffed vine leaves, *boruks*—a delicious crispy pastry stuffed with cheese and fried—aubergines in batter and various other dishes. All of which tasted delicious.

'I'd be quite happy to live on *mezes* for ever,' said Harriet to Suzy, feeling more cheerful, and deciding her imagination was over active.

Suzy agreed. 'There's hardly any need for a main dish.'

'Ah, but then you miss so much.' Philippe joined them at the table and helped himself from the assortment of dishes spread out in the middle. '*Afiyet Olsun*,' he said. 'Good appetite, in Turkish.'

'*Afiyet Olsun*,' they replied with varying degrees of success at the pronunciation.

Everyone was trying to learn Turkish, except Felix. He never made any effort to speak Turkish, either to their Turkish colleagues or anyone else, so Harriet presumed he didn't bother with the patients either. She wished he would try, but in that respect she knew he would be stubbornly English in his attitude.

Harriet had learned quite a few Turkish words, and now she and Halide, sitting next to her at the table, were able to converse quite well in a mixture of English and Turkish.

'Halide will be accompanying you and Barry when you start going out to the villages,' Philippe interrupted Harriet's conversation with Halide. He leaned forward, amber eyes alight with enthusiasm. 'As well as immunisation and vaccination, I want to start a basic health education and hygiene programme. Halide can translate for you. Tuberculosis is a big problem here and——'

'But with all the drugs available for TB——' began Harriet.

'True there's streptomycin and all the related drugs, but there are so many people out there in the villages, and drugs are expensive. Besides, prevention is better than cure, and that's what I'm aiming for.' He looked quite fierce. 'Surely you agree?'

'Of course.' Harriet faltered in front of his explosive passion. 'I . . . I didn't realise it was such a big problem.'

Philippe glowered, his eyes growing dark and reflective. 'Most people don't,' he said. 'This is a half-way country. Half east, half west. Some of the western benefits, and most of the eastern problems.'

Yes, thought Harriet suddenly, that description fits you exactly, Philippe Krir—half east, half west!

Barry sat up, looking interested as Philippe spoke. 'Yep,' he said enthusiastically, 'there's a helluva lot we can do out there.'

'You don't mind working outside the hospital.' Philippe looked directly at Harriet and raised his dark brows questioningly. 'The conditions won't be ideal.'

'I'm a nurse, trained to work under any conditions.' She felt slightly put out to be considered some sort of hot-house species.

'You might be shocked.'

Harriet had the feeling he was trying to unnerve her. 'I expect I shall cope.'

'Expect! I hired you because I thought you *could*.'

'I can and I will cope,' retorted Harriet in a much louder voice than she had intended. 'I have no doubt whatsoever in my abilities.'

'Good to know one of us has no doubts!' came the pithy reply.

Harriet opened her mouth to reply sharply, then closed it. He was baiting her on purpose and she would not rise! Philippe suddenly grinned, confirming her suspicions, and she turned her head haughtily away.

'How are things in the surgical world?' she asked, turning her attention to Felix.

'I need a different operating table,' said Felix. He looked at Philippe. 'When are we going to do something about that?'

'Tomorrow,' replied Philippe quietly. 'I hadn't forgotten. I've managed to bring the appointment with Fatima forward to tomorrow. We should be able to agree on which table to purchase. Perhaps you could glance over the medical catalogues again.'

It seemed to Harriet that Philippe's voice had held a caustic note of reprimand, but Felix didn't appear to notice.

The conversation was interrupted by the cook entering with a large earthenware dish of baked octopus, which he placed on the table. Harriet and Suzy had never eaten octopus before, and both were a little apprehensive. But one mouthful of the baked fish, coated with an exquisite crusty cheese topping, soon dispelled any doubts they might have had. Everyone, including Felix, enthusiastically pronounced the dish fantastic, and the cook disappeared back into the kitchen looking very pleased.

Dinner was nearly over, when Suzy hissed in Harriet's ear, 'I'm going to ask him.' She leaned towards Philippe and put on her most appealing expression. 'May we borrow the minibus and go down into Bodrum tonight?' she asked.

Philippe laughed. 'You needn't flutter your eyelashes,' he teased, 'you know I'm a soft touch.'

'I would never have guessed,' Harriet muttered to Suzy.

But he willingly gave his permission before he left the hospital to return to his private villa, and suggested that everyone off duty should go.

The Turkish girls were not interested, they preferred to watch television and disappeared in the direction of the TV lounge. Halide couldn't go as it was her turn to look after the two post-operative appendicectomy patients. The girls, including Harriet and Suzy, had devised a rota between them, and they all took turns at night duty.

Harriet would have loved to have gone down into Bodrum. She gazed at it now from the terrace outside the dining-room. It looked beautiful at night. Clusters of twinkling lights dotted the hillside, dwarfed by the huge floodlit castle of St Peter. The castle, standing guard at the harbour entrance, looked mysterious and romantic.

Just as she was about to say yes, Felix said, 'I shall be too busy.'

'Come on,' said Suzy, 'you don't want to spend another night in, surely?'

But Felix was adamant. 'I need to go over those catalogues,' he said. 'If we are to make a decision tomorrow on the operating table, I want to be well briefed.'

Harriet hid a happy smile. 'Actually, I've got a bit of a headache,' she said. 'You go on without me.'

Bodrum could wait for another evening. At least with everyone out of the way, she and Felix would be able to have some time to themselves. Philippe had gone back to his own villa in the village of Torba, which Harriet knew was on the other side of the Bodrum peninsular. She would be alone with Felix, at last! How clever of him to think of the catalogues as an excuse.

Barry and Suzy didn't spend long wasting sympathy, and within minutes the sound of the old bus chugging down the mountainside had faded into silence.

Harriet retired to her room in the seraglio with her fictional headache, and waited impatiently until she was sure everyone had gone to their various destinations. Then, leaving the room, she made her way in the darkness past the pool. A low throbbing sound told her that some frogs had taken up residence there. She grinned cheerfully to herself; they must be very determined frogs to come half-way up a mountain and find a pond in the middle of a palace!

Pausing for a moment on the edge of the courtyard, she looked back, and sighed contentedly. Although she didn't want to admit it, and would never have done so to Philippe, she was beginning to enjoy the peaceful life of the seraglio. Now, as she stood silent and watchful, the intricate mosaics glimmered beneath a pale crescent moon, slung low in a star-spangled sky. The opaque wall lamps, set behind the graceful fluted arches surrounding the courtyard, threw a mottled pattern of light on the water, which sighed and shifted in a soft warm breeze. Still smiling happily, she softly closed the brass fretted door behind her, and went into the main body of the ancient palace.

She found Felix sitting at the desk in his room. He and Barry had rooms in what had once been the young princes' suite. They were every bit as luxurious as the girls' rooms, but decorated in a more masculine way. The walls were hung with prayer rugs of every size and colour imaginable, each one with the distinctive pattern of a minaret, which when placed on the floor was intended to face Mecca.

'Hello, darling.' Crossing the room swiftly, she bent down and kissed the back of his neck.

'I thought you had a headache?' Felix looked up in surprise.

'No, of course not. I thought you wanted me to stay behind with you, so I . . .' her voice trailed away. He really *was* reading medical equipment catalogues. Felix had meant what he had said.

Felix wasn't the best interpreter of expressions, but even he could see that disappointment was written all over her face. He stood up and put his arms around her. 'Oh, darling,' he said quickly, and kissed her, 'you misunderstood me.'

'Yes, I did,' said Harriet. The happy mood evaporated in an instant. Even his kiss was absent-minded, and she was painfully aware that over her shoulder he had one eye on the catalogues. 'I know we are keeping our engagement a secret, but I didn't expect our relationship to disintegrate altogether.'

She hadn't intended to say that, the words just slipped out. What she wanted to say, but dared not, was, Felix, stay close to me, I'm afraid

I'm attracted to Philippe Krir and it frightens me.

Felix laughed. 'What a crazy girl you are,' he said. 'You're over-reacting. Of course our relationship hasn't disintegrated, it's just on "hold" for a while.'

'You can say that again,' muttered Harriet, wishing she felt more reassured. 'I never see you alone.'

'There will be plenty of other times.' Felix put her away from him, and sat down again at his desk. 'Sorry, darling, but I really do have to look through these catalogues very carefully.' Harriet was hurt by the impatience of his voice. 'If I don't know exactly what I want by tomorrow, Philippe will make the decision for me.' His voice hardened. 'He likes to think he's running the whole show, you know.'

'Well, he is, isn't he?' said Harriet. She had been about to add that it was Philippe's hospital, when Felix interrupted her.

'He is *not* going to run the theatres if I have anything to do with it. I know he's a physician, an anaesthetist and a surgeon. A jack of all trades! But theatres should be designed and run by specialist surgeons like me, and I intend to see that I have the major say.'

'Oh, Felix!' Harriet was suddenly exasperated beyond measure. She'd heard that sort of hierarchical argument so many times before. 'Why can't you just work together, like two sensible human beings!'

'Because I am the senior surgeon,' replied Felix haughtily, 'the senior specialist of the hospital. That's the way it always is.'

'In England, perhaps,' said Harriet crossly, 'but even there, it's a myth being clung on to tenaciously by egotistical surgeons, frightened of losing their prestige. One doctor is no better than another!' She surprised herself at her words. She had often thought them, but never actually uttered the opinion before.

'Goodnight, Harriet. When I need a lecture on the medical profession, I'll tell you!' There was no mistaking the icy dismissal in his voice.

'Goodnight, Felix.' Her tone was equally icy.

Leaving the room swiftly, she banged the door noisily behind her, venting her anger on it. Why did Felix have to be so arrogant sometimes? But more than his arrogance, another thing was bothering her. Since he had taken her engagement ring back, Felix appeared to have dismissed her from his mind altogether, and that, combined with her troubled feelings about Philippe, threw her into a panic. The feeling of freedom she'd relished at the beginning had disappeared; now she wanted reassurance that they were still in love. A ring shouldn't make any difference, she told herself, but the love, which she had always taken for granted, was now stretched to breaking point. It was something she had never expected to happen, and a dull ache of unhappiness filled her heart.

Wandering aimlessly through the palace, she reached the large outer courtyard. Wishing that she had gone with Suzy and Barry, she leaned against an arch, looking at the pools of darkness in the shadows. Philippe had told them that once this had been the place where the Sultan's people would gather for shows of horsemanship or camel wrestling. Now it was silent and empty in the moonlight, and in spite of the warmth of the night Harriet felt cold and alone.

The large gateway was wide open. No one seemed to worry about such things as burglars in Turkey. A bit different from London, thought Harriet, and passed beneath the high carved archway of the main door. Once outside, she stood looking at the lights of the town below. If it hadn't been so far, she would have walked, but as it was she had to content herself with a stroll to a projecting overhang of rock on the other side of the road.

The rock projected out further than she had realised, and she was able to get a wonderful view of the coastline stretching way beyond the actual bay of Bodrum itself. Far away, in the velvet blackness of night, she could see beads of lights where coastal villages clung to the narrow strips of shoreline at the foot of the mountains. And out at sea, a mass of green and red lights bobbed about, as fishermen went about their nightly business. But in spite of the beauty before her, nothing could dispel the overwhelming feeling of loneliness.

Lost in thought, she didn't notice the lights of a vehicle making its way up the mountainside, until it rounded the sharp bend in front of the palace. Then the bright lights lit her lonely figure, dazzling her with their brilliance.

'Don't move.' The words were shouted at her urgently as the vehicle screeched to a halt. The next moment Philippe was at her side. 'Come here,' he ordered roughly, pulling her arm, trying to lead her away from the edge.

Harriet snatched her arm free. Philippe Krir was the last person she wanted to see. 'I'm looking at the view,' she said, adding sarcastically, 'What on earth did you think, that I was going to jump?'

With a quick movement she stepped back to her original position. But as she did so the earth beneath her feet moved and, cursing volubly, Philippe grabbed her, hauling her back just in time. Horrified now, Harriet realised she had been standing on a huge overhanging boulder, which now, almost as if in slow motion, broke away from the edge and went bouncing in thundering leaps and bounds down the mountainside. It was a long time before the crashing stopped, and finally there was silence once more. A silence broken only by frightened bleating and clanking of bells, as the mountain goats scurried about. The falling boulder had rudely disturbed their sleep.

'I hope the goats are all right,' said Harriet in a croaky voice. Her mouth was suddenly dry with fear as she realised what might have happened to her, but for Philippe.

'Of course they're all right,' said Philippe, matter-of-factly. 'They live on the mountain, and they have a lot more sense than a good many humans I could mention!'

Suddenly Harriet was aware that he was still holding her very tightly, much too tightly in fact, and that they were both breathing fast.

'I'm . . . I'm sorry. I didn't realise it was dangerous.' A shuddering sigh escaped her lips, and instinctively she leaned against the solid comfort of his body.

Gently Philippe moved her further away from the edge, on to the side of the road, but he still held her close. 'It's my fault,' he said huskily. 'I should have had a notice put there. The locals all know it's dangerous, but I had forgotten about my English guests.'

Harriet looked up. She could just make out his face in the pale light of the moon, it was strong and reassuring. It seemed the most natural thing in the world when his lips touched hers in a gentle caress, then moved to her temple. Her feeling of loneliness disappeared, and without thinking she slid her arms around his comforting warmth. Through the solid wall of bone and muscle, she could feel his heartbeat. It was thundering at the same tempo as her own. When his lips sought hers again, she responded as naturally as a flower opens to the sun. His kisses deepened in intensity, and suddenly Harriet felt as if she'd been set on fire. Philippe's lips had been the match to her unstable emotions and, reckless now, she craved for all his ardour. He, in turn, tightened his hold, pulling her closer and closer until she felt her body answering the fierce heat of his desire.

The lights of the returning minibus brought Harriet back to reality. With a gasp she put her hand to her burning lips, and staggered a few steps away from Philippe. 'I'm sorry,' she gasped.

She could hardly believe the passionate kiss had just happened. What on earth must he think of her? But, in the midst of her confusion and embarrassment, it struck her forcibly that kissing Philippe was quite, quite different from kissing Felix. Nervously she ran the tip of her tongue over her bruised and burning lips, and backed further away. 'I shouldn't have done that,' she whispered.

'Why not?' Philippe gave a deep, husky chuckle. He was not in the least embarrassed. 'I thought you prided yourself on being an emancipated western woman. And, that being the case, what is so wrong with one little kiss?'

'I shouldn't have because——' She stopped abruptly. She'd been about to blurt out, because

I'm engaged to Felix. Although she knew she could have added for good measure—because it wasn't just one little kiss, it was the most earth-shattering kiss I've ever had!

'Because of what?' Philippe pressed her to continue, his tone wry with amusement.

'Because you are my boss,' said Harriet thinking quickly, and saying the first remotely plausible thing that came into her head. 'And I have this rule. I try never to get involved with people I work with.'

Before he could stop her, she broke away completely and ran across to the gateway. Once through the main courtyard, she didn't stop running until she had reached the safety of her room in the seraglio. But his answering words followed her, ringing all the way down the long corridors. He had thrown back his head, roaring with laughter at her words.

'Prim little English miss,' he called after her. 'Since when does one little kiss signal involvement?'

Lying on her bed, listening to the sleepy croaking of the frogs in the courtyard pool, she reflected on his taunting words. It was perfectly true, of course, one kiss did not signal involvement, so what was she worried about? She had enjoyed harmless flirtations before her engagement to Felix. But this was different, the memory of that one kiss was disturbing. Had it really meant nothing at all to him? Suddenly, she felt chilled to the bone, and her stomach tied itself into tight little knots. What a fool she was. *Of course* it meant nothing, why should it?

She heard Suzy come back, clattering noisily across the courtyard, humming loudly and hopelessly out of tune. She went straight to her own room, for which Harriet was thankful.

Much, much later Harriet was still wide awake, watching the stars through the fretted bars of her windows. 'One kiss does not signal involvement,' she whispered fiercely. Why, then, was that one kiss still burning her lips, and why then couldn't she banish it from her mind?

Eventually she decided that she must have responded so emotionally because Philippe had caught her on the rebound. That was the reason, of course it was. She was hurt and upset at Felix's apparent lack of interest in her, and had turned with undue alacrity to the first man to show her tenderness. That was why she had kissed him back so passionately. It was nothing to worry about, nothing at all, she told herself airily. One kiss does not signal involvement—quite true! What a pity, though, that the one kiss had to be from Philippe Krir. Tiredness at last began to make her thoughts hazy. Turning over, she buried her face in the pillow.

'A kiss from anyone else would have been so much easier to forget,' she grumbled sleepily.

CHAPTER FOUR

NEXT morning at breakfast Suzy and Barry regaled them with stories of their exploration the night before. They had both fallen in love with Bodrum.

'Look at this,' said Suzy, through a mouthful of bread and honey. 'A guide book, showing all the local bays and beaches, and places of historical interest.'

'Crikey, but she's an avid collector,' commented Barry, raising his eyebrows in mock despair. 'If I hadn't restrained her, she'd have bought every book in the shop!'

'We haven't come for a holiday,' Felix commented dourly, as Suzy thrust the book excitedly under his nose.

'If you think I've come all the way to Turkey only to miss the sights, then you are very much mistaken,' said Suzy positively.

'It would be silly to miss such an opportunity,' Harriet agreed. She smiled at Felix encouragingly, willing him to relax for a moment or two, and to think of something else other than medicine. 'I'd really love to see Troy.'

'Glad to hear you say so,' said Barry with a pleased grin, 'because I've arranged to hire a jeep next time I go down into Bodrum. I thought if we all shared the expenses, whoever is off duty can take it and go out sightseeing, or whatever else it is they want to do. We're a bit stuck here, on top of this mountain, and we can't rely on borrowing the minibus all the time.'

'Count me in,' said Harriet enthusiastically. 'Just tell me how much I owe you when it's fixed up.'

There was no need for Suzy to answer, she'd already made up her mind, but Felix was dubious. 'I'll think about it,' he conceded finally, 'but today I've got more important things on my mind.'

Almost as if he had been waiting in the wings for a cue to make his entrance, Philippe arrived. Close on his heels was a very glamorous, dark-haired young woman.

'Madame Fatima Mascari,' he said, waving a hand in her direction before proceeding to introduce them to her one by one.

Harriet liked her immediately. Her smile was open and unaffected, and she seemed genuinely pleased to meet them. She looks very nice, thought Harriet, and *very* young. She wondered what had happened to her husband. She must have been widowed at a very early age. At the same time, she tried to ignore the disturbing twinge of envy that suddenly twisted viciously within her.

Fatima and Philippe were a handsome pair.

They were both dark, and strikingly good-looking. In fact, thought Harriet, they were strangely similar in an undefinable way. Harriet looked at Fatima's slim, svelte figure in her expensively cut linen suit, and wished she was wearing something more glamorous than her nurse's uniform.

'How are you, Harriet? You had me quite worried last night!'

At Philippe's words, every eye in the room swivelled in Harriet's direction. Inwardly seething, she nevertheless managed what she hoped would pass for a sweet smile. 'I'm fine,' she said, praying that the conversation would move on to hospital matters.

It was not to be. 'Philippe was worried. What on earth for?' asked Felix.

'You didn't tell them?' Philippe raised his eyebrows. There was just the merest suspicion of an amused glint in his eye and Harriet cursed him beneath her breath. The wretched man was enjoying every minute!

'Tell us what?' asked Suzy. 'Come on, I'm all agog!'

'You always are,' teased Barry, 'but come on, Harriet, even I'm curious.'

'There's nothing much to tell,' said Harriet quickly, anxious to get off the subject as soon as possible. 'I slipped, and Philippe very kindly picked me up.'

'I don't call nearly falling off the edge of the

mountain nothing,' said Philippe, and went on to explain exactly what had happened. Then he looked Harriet directly in the eyes and said, 'Of course, I must give Harriet full marks for maintaining her cool. It must be that British stiff upper lip. Any other girl would have collapsed in a heap in my arms!'

'I definitely would,' said Suzy with a flirtatious giggle.

Harriet glowered at her, and studiously kept her eyes averted from Philippe's amused gaze.

Barry didn't help much either. 'Your lips don't look a bit stiff to me,' he said, and everyone roared with laughter.

Except Felix who looked rather put out. 'You should have come and told me,' he said, 'you knew I was there.'

'Why?' demanded Harriet, fast losing her patience. 'I didn't fall, only nearly. If I *had* fallen, someone else would have told you all!'

'Harriet, I was only trying to be helpful. There's no need——'

'Anyway,' said Harriet pointedly, 'I knew you were busy with your medical catalogues.'

'Ah, yes,' said Felix, his mind immediately switching back to medical matters. He smiled at Fatima. 'We have much to talk about, Madame Mascari. I am ready for our meeting whenever you are.'

Harriet wondered if Felix would have dropped the subject so quickly if he had known of

Philippe's passionate kiss. Probably, she thought gloomily. She looked at Philippe, standing so near and yet so far away, and her heart upped its tempo several notches. And, against her better judgement, the twinge of envy became worse, twisting like a sharp knife in her stomach, as she compared her own fair-skinned, green-eyed appearance to Fatima's luxurious, sultry beauty. It was no use, she had to concede that Suzy was probably right. It was inevitable that the widow should have designs on Philippe, and who could possibly blame her for that?

Her idle musings were jerked to a halt by Madame Fatima's voice. 'Please do not stand on ceremony,' she said to Felix. 'Why on earth Philippe has introduced me as Madame Fatima Mascari, I cannot think.' She gave Philippe a teasing squeeze of the arm, her dark eyes twinkling. 'He knows perfectly well that everyone calls me Fatima, and so must all of you. I'm sure I'll be seeing a lot of you. I'm often here to see how my pet project is coming along.'

'Huh! and to see how her pet, Philippe, is coming along as well, I expect,' Suzy muttered from behind Harriet.

It was rather a loud mutter and, afraid that Philippe would hear, Harriet administered a sharp kick on Suzy's shins. It had the desired effect, and after pulling a rude face at Harriet Suzy subsided into mutinous silence. The introductions over, Felix, Philippe and Fatima disappeared in the direction of Philippe's office.

Harriet watched them go, and wondered if the others had noticed how Felix had turned on the charm, as only he knew how. His blue eyes were sparkling as he bent his head, attentively listening to whatever it was that Fatima was saying. For the second time that morning, she felt a vicious stab of jealous envy. This is ridiculous, she told herself firmly. You're getting quite neurotic!

Suzy went off to take over from the night nurse. 'With any luck our two patients should be well enough to go home the day after tomorrow,' she announced as she left. 'Let's keep our fingers crossed and hope we have some more surgical emergencies, otherwise I can see Felix will go stark raving mad with inactivity!'

'That's one thing that never drives me mad—inactivity,' said Barry comfortably, as he and Harriet walked along the corridor towards the suite of rooms that served as their outpatient clinic. 'I can be quite happy doing absolutely nothing at all.' As he spoke, he suddenly bent over double and groaned.

At first Harriet thought he was clowning around, but then quickly saw that he wasn't. She stopped and helped him stand upright.

'What is it?' She was concerned now, he had gone very pale and beads of perspiration were standing out on his face.

'I don't know.' He groaned again, and

doubled up with pain. 'Well, yes, I think I do,' he said when he regained his breath. 'I think maybe I shouldn't have eaten all those fried mussels last night! You start the clinic, I'll join you later.' He disappeared down the corridor at a rapid pace, bent double and groaning dramatically.

Harriet watched him and grinned unsympathetically. 'Fried mussels, on top of baked octopus! No wonder you have pains in your stomach,' she shouted after him.

Halide was already in the clinic when Harriet arrived. Ali had delivered two bus loads of patients, and they sat quietly in orderly rows on the chairs placed ready for them. By now, Harriet had got used to the uniform dress of the women—voluminous baggy trousers, heads covered by scarves usually pulled partially across their faces in a gesture of modesty. As always they were surrounded by a sea of children, usually very clean and tidy. But this morning, Harriet noticed there was quite a large contingent who could only be described as distinctly grubby.

'A different type of patient this morning,' she remarked to Halide.

'Our first gipsy patients,' Halide replied. 'I'm afraid there might be difficulties, as they didn't want to come.'

'Then we will deal with them first,' said Harriet decisively, and then she told Halide that the two of them would have to run the clinic that morning as Barry was not well. 'Too many fried mussels,' she grinned in answer to Halide's worried look.

Halide continued to look worried. 'Maybe Philippe Krir should look at him,' she said.

'Oh, no. He'll be joining us in half an hour.' Harriet was unconcerned; Barry hadn't seemed that ill.

But they had finished the clinic, there was still no sign of Barry. The two girls walked back towards the dining-room for lunch, both exhausted. It had been a hard morning's work, and Harriet had used every psychological ploy she'd ever been taught. It had been difficult to overcome the gipsies' innate fear of officialdom.

'We can tell Barry we won't be needing him in future,' she said to Halide with a tired grin as they entered the hospital dining-room for lunch.

Halide pulled a face. 'Just as well,' she said, passing Harriet a note which was propped upon the dining-room table. It was from Barry saying he didn't think he would be able to make it for the afternoon clinic, and that he'd see them tomorow, if he survived!

'Oh, dear, perhaps I'd better go and see him,' said Harriet anxiously, folding the note.

'See who?' Philippe appeared with Fatima and Felix in tow. Felix was looking very pleased with himself, and gave Harriet a beaming smile. Obviously all had gone to his liking.

'Barry is ill,' said Harriet, smiling briefly back at Felix, and passing the note over to Philippe. 'He ate fried mussels last night, and they seem to have disagreed with him.'

Philippe took the proffered note. 'I'll go and look at him,' he said scowling, and disappeared, muttering under his breath, 'Fried mussels, of all the things to eat. A doctor should know better!'

They were half-way through lunch when Philippe reappeared and announced that Barry would probably be sick for several days. 'A surfeit of gluttony,' was his diagnosis, 'the cure for which is plenty of boiled water, and kaolin.'

'Poor Barry,' said Harriet. 'I hope you were kind to him.' Philippe had sounded rather fierce.

'I'm always kind,' he said, his mouth curving in a taunting lopsided smile that did strange things to her pulse. Then he asked Halide something in Turkish.

She replied at length, and as she spoke Harriet was uncomfortably aware that Philippe was watching her intently. She felt her cheeks beginning to colour. I *won't* blush, she told herself fiercely. I must stop acting like a gauche schoolgirl whenever he looks at me! But, glancing at Philippe through her lashes, she couldn't help remembering how his lips had felt on hers.

His mind, however, was very much work-orientated. 'Halide tells me that you gained the confidence of the gipsy women,' he said matter-of-factly. 'I'm glad, because now I shall send you and Halide to the outlying districts alone, while Barry can finish setting up the paediatric ward. I need some specialist advice from him, and that way I shall be able to achieve my goals more quickly.'

'Philippe, what a slave driver you are!' reprimanded Fatima with a chuckle. She laid a fond hand on his sleeve.

He said nothing, merely grinned back at her, and his long brown fingers patted her hand. It was an intimate, tender gesture, conveying an easy knowledge and affection. They know each other very well, thought Harriet, averting her eyes quickly, very well indeed! How foolish she was even bothering to remember that fleeting kiss. He had laughed at her reaction last night, and would laugh even more if he knew she was still thinking about it. She had proudly told him she was a western woman, and here she was still mulling over one little kiss like a moonstruck idiot!

Determinedly concentrating on peeling an orange for dessert, and trying not to look in Philippe's direction, Harriet was unaware at first that Felix was speaking to her. 'And so we are going first to Izmir, and then perhaps on to Istanbul,' he said.

'We?' asked Harriet.

Felix was taking her to Izmir! Suddenly she felt light-hearted with happiness: she would be with

Felix, away from Philippe, and everything would be all right. Everything, including her emotions, would fall back into the old familiar pattern.

'Fatima and I,' emphasised Felix. 'We are going to choose the new operating table. Haven't you been listening to a word I've been saying?'

'Sorry,' Harriet's impulsively optimistic hopes were dashed by his reply. 'I didn't hear everything you said,' she murmured awkwardly.

Looking up, she was aware once more that Philippe's all-seeing eyes were watching her. She hoped he couldn't read her mind, but had a nasty feeling that he found it all too easy. Tightening her lips, she stared back at him defiantly, green eyes flashing emerald fire. Philippe, however, didn't drop his eyes as she'd hoped, and instead she lost her nerve and switched her gaze to Felix.

'We are leaving this afternoon.' Felix sounded satisfied with his morning's work, and Harriet knew her earlier assumption had been correct. Negotiations had gone his way. 'It may take several days; the roads are slow, and we may not be able to telex all the companies from Izmir.'

'Supposing there are any surgical cases?' interrupted Suzy.

'Barry or I will do them.' said Philippe. 'We are both quite capable, although, of course——' he paused a moment and looked across at

Felix '—we are not as good as Felix.'

Harriet suddenly realised that Philippe had sized up Felix, and taken note of his inbuilt prejudices and his sometimes inflated ego.

Suzy had obviously drawn the same conclusion, and said a trifle maliciously, 'You'll have to be careful, Felix will give you marks out of ten when he returns!'

'I shall do no such thing.' Felix had the grace to look embarrassed. 'In a country like this, where the nearest surgeon is ten hours away by road, a doctor should be able to turn his hand to anything.'

'Yes, but would *you*?' Harriet found herself saying. Felix was always drumming it into everyone that he was a surgeon, nothing else, and that he was very different from being a mere doctor!

'Of course,' he snapped, looking mortified that anyone should doubt him.

'Harriet, I'm surprised at you! Fancy being so unkind as to needle your . . .' Philippe hesitated, before continuing, 'your colleague, Felix.'

Harriet stared at him suspiciously. She could have sworn he'd been about to say something other than colleague. The topaz eyes were bland and enigmatic. Harriet lowered her gaze. 'Yes, it was mean of me,' she agreed. 'Sorry, Felix.'

'Apologies accepted,' said Felix, 'although I must say you do seem very edgy today, Harriet.'

'A bit tired, I expect,' murmured Harriet and

after that the subject was dropped, much to her relief.

After lunch Fatima and Felix departed in Fatima's sleek white Mercedes. Suzy and Harriet, in the company of Philippe, went out into the outer courtyard to watch them depart.

'They look like a couple of film stars,' commented Suzy, watching golden-haired Felix, in a pale linen suit, complete with dark reflector sunglasses, stowing his cases in the boot. 'He's blond, beautiful and sexy, and she's dark, beautiful and sexy!'

Harriet laughed uneasily. 'True,' she said, 'they do look like something out of a glossy magazine.'

Felix was good looking, but her heart felt heavy at the sight of him. He didn't stir her, or send prickles racing down her spine. Stubbornly she told herself that everything would be all right if only she could run to him, fling her arms around him and kiss him goodbye, or, better still, plead with him not to leave her. Instead, she had to content herself with standing under the shady arches surrounding the baking hot courtyard, shielding her eyes against the glare from the stones as she waved a nonchalant goodbye, an unsuspecting Suzy at her side.

As the Mercedes drove out through the gateway, she found her gaze automatically drawn towards Philippe. His eyes were resting on her face with watchful scrutiny, and she was struck again by the powerful aura surrounding him. She wanted to tear her gaze away, but she couldn't. Instead she stared back. Like a rabbit hypnotised by a snake, she thought, feeling angry at her lack of willpower. Making a determined effort, she turned, and started to walk away.

Suzy followed her, and Philippe strode past them. 'It's not fair,' said Suzy. 'No man should be allowed to be so sexy!'

'Sexy?' queried Harriet, feigning amazement. But her gaze watched the muscles rippling beneath his cream silk shirt almost greedily, as she relived the moment of being held against that rock-hard body.

'Terrifically sexy,' said Suzy with a sigh, her eyes riveted on Philippe. 'To think we are under the same roof as two of the sexiest men on earth. Which one do you fancy?'

'Neither,' replied Harriet with a vehemence that surprised Suzy. She looked at her watch. 'I must dash,' she said, and fled before Suzy could ask her to explain her anti-male feelings.

She was glad to reach the clinic. Keeping busy with the next batch of mothers and children was a good way of forgetting both Felix and Philippe. In fact, she found it surprisingly easy to relegate Felix to the back of her mind; even the fact that she wouldn't see him for perhaps a week or more now seemed insignificant. But relegating Philippe to the same place, however, proved much more difficult.

A task not helped by the fact that the patients and Halide continually talked about him, with something closely akin to rapt adoration. Although she couldn't understand half of what was being said, Harriet began to feel that she would scream if Philippe Krir's name was mentioned one more time!

The next moment, however, she was wishing Philippe was around. Halide ushered a young mother and four children under the age of five into the cubicle. They were all well cared for, but the second youngest child, aged about two, was very unwell. Halide didn't need to interpret for Harriet to know the mother was worried to death. Her enormous brown eyes were clouded with worry, and she thrust the child at Harriet as soon as they entered the cubicle.

Harriet immediately swung into top gear, and gently laid the small boy on the couch. 'Ask her when he started to be unwell,' she told Halide. She took his temperature; as she expected it was sky high.

'The mother says he had a cold last week,' Halide informed her, 'and then he started croaking like a frog and being like this. He can't swallow very well, and he can't breathe when he lies down.'

'Dysphagia and dyspnoea following upper respiratory tract infection,' muttered Harriet under her breath, hastily writing up a hospital record card in the child's name. Halide looked over her shoulder, as she wrote the unfamiliar words. 'Those are the medical names for difficulty in swallowing and breathing,' explained Harriet. 'He has what is called orthopnoea, which means he can only breathe relatively easily when he sits up.'

'What is the matter with him?' Halide looked at the sick child soberly.

'I think it is acute epiglottitis,' said Harriet. 'See how badly he is dribbling. Now, if you can help me, we need to persuade him to open his mouth and then we can have a look.'

Halide nodded. 'You'll want this,' she said, reaching for a tongue depressor from the instrument tray.

Harriet shook her head. 'Not this time. One thing you must always remember,' she impressed upon Halide, 'is that in cases like this, you must never use a tongue depressor. If you do, you can cause a laryngospasm which could completely obstruct the airway. Then you would have real trouble on your hands.'

Halide nodded attentively, and together with Harriet gently propped up their small patient. He was feeling too ill to make much protest, and obediently opened his mouth when asked to by Halide.

Harriet looked carefully down the child's throat. Sure enough, the pencil-slim beam of light easily picked up the epiglottis. It was enlarged and cherry-red in colour.

'Here, have a look,' she said to Halide, and

then beckoned the mother over too, so that she could see and understand the problem.

'What shall we do?' asked Halide. 'Shall I go and get Barry? It will have to be Barry. Philippe has gone out this afternoon.'

Harriet thought quickly. She was confident they had caught it in the early stages, and an antibiotic like amoxycillin would do the trick. In England the child might have been admitted on to the ward for continuous observation, but here, although they had a ward, they had no beds as yet, so that was not an option. There was no alternative, the child would have to go home.

'No need to get Barry,' she told Halide. 'We can manage. This is the sort of case you will have to deal with on your own, after we have returned to England. It's a common childhood complaint, and usually responds very well to treatment. Will you explain to the mother that I am going to give him an injection of antibiotic now, and some syrup to take away. She must give him one spoonful of the syrup three times a day, starting with one spoonful tonight, then start the daily dose tomorrow.' Harriet paused, then added, 'Oh, and take a careful note of where she lives. Someone from the hospital will come down and see the child later.'

'But how?' said Halide. 'We don't visit. They always come here.'

'We will visit this time,' said Harriet firmly, 'and if *you* deal with a case like this, then you must always follow it up yourself.' Halide nodded, her black eyes round with gravity. 'Oh, and another thing, tell the mother to prop him up with plenty of pillows and keep him in bed, and give him lots of cool water to drink to bring the fever down.'

While Halide was busily relaying all this information to the mother, Harriet drew up the correct dose of ammoxil injection. When they had finished with the little boy, and had duly vaccinated the other children of the family, Harriet went to find Ali.

'I would like a family taken home in isolation from the rest of the patients,' she told him. There was no point in passing on infection unnecessarily.

'Yes, Doctor,' said Ali. In spite of her preoccupation with the child, Harriet smiled. Ali was convinced that all the English were doctors, and nothing could persuade him otherwise.

Getting Ali and the family organised took some time, and by the time they were finishing with the remainder of their small patients for the afternoon, the clinic was running well over an hour late. So late, in fact, that on his return Philippe strolled into the treatment area to find out what was causing the hold-up.

Halide dropped everything at the sight of Philippe, which annoyed Harriet intensely. Wasn't it bad enough that she felt like dropping everything whenever he hove into view, without Halide actually doing it! Her defensive mechanism was to adopt her most officious, 'dragon of a nurse' air, the one she usually kept for flirtatious male patients.

'Halide,' she snapped at the surprised girl, 'please tidy up that instrument tray before the next patient comes in.'

Then she busied herself quite unnecessarily rearranging everything in the cubicle. 'Excuse me,' she said, practically tipping Philippe into the rubbish bin along with a handful of paper tissues, 'but we're rather busy.'

Philippe was not in the least deterred. Her officiousness rolled off him like water off a duck's back. 'Problems?' he asked laconically.

'No,' said Harriet firmly, flashing Halide a look that dared her to utter a word of contradiction. 'Now if you *will* excuse us.'

'Are you sending me away?' He raised his sooty eyebrows, and shot her a wickedly sensual smile that turned her knees to water. Then, to make matters worse, he moved closer.

Harriet swallowed hard. Philippe was standing right in front of her, and her legs were giving a realistic impression of unset jelly! 'Yes,' she said very loudly. If he doesn't go soon, I'll fall over, she thought in panic.

'I should have guessed you could be a real virago,' he said, still smiling broadly. 'I'll see you both later.'

'I would never dare do that,' said Halide after he'd gone, awestruck at what she considered the enormity of Harriet dismissing her boss.

'We have a job to do,' said Harriet abruptly, wishing she could act normally when Philippe was around, and that she had mentioned the child with epiglottitis.

She was tired, and although she didn't admit it to Halide, she was beginning to worry. Had she done the right thing in sending that small boy back home? What were the home circumstances like? Would the mother do as she had been told? Supposing the larynx became completely obstructed by the oedematous epiglottis? A whole host of worries suddenly flooded over her, and a cold, hard lump of anxiety lodged in her chest. Somehow she would get down to see the child that night, otherwise she knew she would never sleep.

'Oh, we didn't tell Philippe about the boy with epiglottitis,' said Halide, echoing Harriet's thoughts.

'I'll tell Barry,' said Harriet, 'he's the paediatric expert.' And the less time I spend with Philippe, the better, she added silently.

The curtain swished back and Halide ushered the last but one family in. Automatically Harriet switched on her welcoming smile.

'Yes,' she said to Halide. 'Barry will probably be well enough to go down to Bodrum with me tonight.'

If not, she would go alone. Trips with Philippe were definitely out of the question. His deliberately sensual smile flashed before her eyes again and she shivered. She didn't trust that man as far as she could throw him! And what about you, her conscience taunted. Could you guarantee to behave in an exemplary manner?

CHAPTER FIVE

AS SOON as the clinic was finished, Harriet dashed off to see Barry, but to her disappointment he still didn't feel well enough to go out.

'Sorry, love, better stay near the bathroom,' he said.

One glance at his greenish pallor was enough to convince her that he was probably right. 'Don't worry about it.' Harriet tried to sound cheerful, but failed miserably. 'I suppose I'd better tell Philippe.'

But Barry suggested a better alternative. 'Why bother Philippe?' he said. 'You can drive, so borrow the minibus and go down on your own.' He grinned reassuringly. 'You know what kids are like, down one minute and up the next. You've done all the right things, I'm sure you've caught it in time.'

'Yes, but supposing I was wrong. Suppose I missed something vital,' worried Harriet.

'Rubbish!' Barry said, as he rushed off to the bathroom once more. 'What can you miss when you look down a throat? You're not an idiot!'

Harriet wandered off disconsolately; Barry,

closeted in the bathroom, was not going to be much more help. She made her way to the outer courtyard, hoping there'd be a sign of the minibus or Ali, but there wasn't, so borrowing the bus at the moment was out of the question.

Back in the seraglio she showered, and then sat under the arches of the courtyard in the cool, trying to read a book. A slight breeze made the perfumed air comfortable, but concentration was impossible, and she was glad when Suzy and Halide made their appearance. They brought with them a new arrival to the hospital. Another Turkish girl, whose name was Sofi. She had done some nursing in an English hospital as an auxiliary.

'Philippe Krir, he recruit me in England,' she said proudly in her halting English. 'My mother in Torba, she tell him about me, and he come to find me. I am glad to be back here in Turkey. Is much better than Birmingham.'

'I agree,' said Harriet with a smile.

Leaning back in her chair, she looked around at the peaceful courtyard. The profusion of potted plants and palms moved slightly in the faint breeze. The clear water of the pool was slashed now with vivid pinks and oranges, boiling with colour as it reflected the dying brilliance of the setting sun. With a start of surprise, Harriet realised that she too had begun to like it almost more than England. She felt at ease here, and more at peace than she'd ever felt in London. The only flies in the ointment were her own stupidly mixed emotions where Philippe Krir was concerned!

She told Suzy about the child with epiglottitis and her worries, but Suzy was as bad as Barry. 'Don't worry so much,' she said. 'I would go down with you, but it's my turn on duty tonight.'

The girls changed, then drifted down together towards the dining-room, for the evening meal. Harriet kept her eyes open for any sign of Ali, but he didn't appear and neither did Philippe. After dinner, Suzy went across to the hospital wing for her night duty, and the other girls went to the TV room, leaving Harriet alone.

The minibus still wasn't in the main courtyard, so there was nothing for it but to kick her heels in frustration.

Knowing that Ali often went along to the kitchen for a chat, Harriet went back to the dining-room, reasoning that that way she would catch him as soon as he arrived. She poured herself a cool lemon drink, then wandered out on to the terrace, and leaned against one of the arches. A night sky of purple velvet sparkled with a myriad of diamond pinpricks, and the lights of Bodrum flickered below. The mournful wail of muezzin drifted up the mountainside, and Harriet knew it must be exactly one hour after sunset.

'Do you think this will ever be a proper

hospital, as good as an English one?'

The voice, and the unexpected question, startled her into almost dropping her drink. Turning, she found Philippe standing beside her. The soft leather of his shoes had made no sound as he crossed the marble floor to where she stood.

'Why, yes, of course I do,' she stammered in surprise. 'Whatever makes you ask?'

'Felix thinks not, or so he has told Fatima.' He gave a strained laugh. 'An impossible dream, to use his exact words.'

He leaned on the balustrade beside Harriet, and began to click some silver worry beads with a rapid rhythm through his fingers.

'Well, I think he's quite wrong,' said Harriet. 'Of course it will be a proper hospital and I think it will be one of the best in Turkey, because you will make it so.' Impulsively she reached out and touched his arm. 'I never imagined you doubting yourself,' she said wonderingly.

'There's a lot you don't know about me, Harriet,' he said sombrely. He turned towards her. 'And there is even more I'd like to know about you.'

Harriet felt the familiar blush begin to steal across her cheeks. 'Well, I——' she began, desperately searching for something suitably non-committal to say.

Philippe swore, the expletive made Harriet jump nervously. He shrugged expressively. 'It's been a damned trying day—so much bureaucracy to contend with.'

He looked down at her slim fingers still resting on his arm, and Harriet hurriedly started to remove her hand. In her confusion she had forgotten it was still there. But before she could remove it altogether, a large, warm hand softly closed over hers and held it in place. Harriet swallowed hard. I mustn't panic, she told herself firmly; I mustn't betray how his touch affects me.

'It's the same in every country,' she heard a voice she hardly recognised as her own saying coolly. She paused and then asked, 'Did Felix manage to order the operating table in Izmir?'

Philippe let out his breath in an expression of exasperation, and let go of her hand. 'No, Felix is determined to have the best that money can buy. He has twisted Fatima around his little finger and convinced her that what we need is a hi-tech table.'

'But surely you want the best as well?' Harriet surreptitiously put a little distance between them, and instantly felt safer. The conversation was safer too—familiar territory, nice impersonal hospital matters.

The silver worry beads glinted in the moonlight as Philippe flicked them with an abruptly vicious movement. 'This hospital is going to be for basic medical care,' he said sharply. 'That is what the people here need. Of course we'll do many types of operations, appendicectomies, trauma surgery, hernias, varicose veins, congenital abnormalities on children when possible—there is a never-ending list of possibilities. But what I can't seem to make Felix understand is that we shall never do coronary artery bypasses, or complicated vascular surgery. We must get our priorities in order.'

He thumped the balustrade angrily, and Harriet, deducing that he and Felix must have had a blazing row, deemed it prudent to remain silent.

Suddenly Philippe turned towards her, and taking a couple of paces closer towered above her. 'How well do you know Felix?' he demanded abruptly.

Harriet took a step backwards, but realised as she did so that it was in the wrong direction. All she had succeeded in doing was cornering herself at the far end of the balustrade, so that Philippe had a clear view of her face.

'How well? Oh, we . . . er . . .' Harriet fumbled for the right words. 'We've worked together for three years,' she said at last, rather lamely.

'Yes, yes, I know that.' He sounded impatient. 'But as a man, do you know him as a man?'

By now Harriet was sure her face must be scarlet with guilt, and cursed the fact that Felix had ever persuaded her to deceive Philippe. She wondered what he would say if she told him they were engaged, and that she did know Felix very well. Or did she? Suddenly she wondered. Felix had become like a stranger to her in such a short space of time, so could she have really have known him that well? For one insane moment, Harriet was on the verge of telling Philippe the truth, but then she saw his face as the moon slid out from behind a bank of cloud. It was stern and cold, and a shiver of fear flicked through her.

'Why?' she asked at last.

'Because, I think perhaps I made a mistake,' said Philippe, his voice heavy with concern. 'I shouldn't have brought him here, he's too self-centred. He doesn't understand what I'm trying to do.'

A loyalty born of habit made Harriet defend Felix. 'Give him time,' she said, 'he's been working in hi-tech hospitals all his life. It's bound to be difficult for him to adjust.'

'Very noble of you to stand up for him,' snapped Philippe bad-temperedly. 'But you, Suzy and Barry seemed to have managed the transition without having nervous breakdowns. Or, even worse, causing me to have one in the process!'

'You, having a nervous breakdown?' Harriet suddenly began to laugh. The idea was so ridiculous.

Philippe shot her a distinctly annoyed look,

then turned and stared moodily down at the lights of Bodrum. When he spoke, it was in a strangely subdued tone. 'The really worrying thing is that he is giving Fatima impracticable ideas. I don't want her to be disappointed.'

Harriet felt a dull ache of resentment at the mention of Fatima. It was obvious that Philippe cared for her very much. She decided it was time to change the subject, and swallowing her misgivings told Philippe about the child with epiglottitis.

The words were hardly out of her mouth before Philippe had grasped her arm, and was trundling her at a brisk pace towards the large outer courtyard. 'We'll both go right away,' he said, opening the door of his jeep as soon as they got to it.

'Oh, but . . . I didn't mean for you to go,' protested Harriet. 'I can drive the jeep—if I could just go down to satisfy myself that everything is all right.'

'What the hell do you think I'm here for?' Philippe plonked her, still protesting, into the jeep, then swung his lithe frame beside her. 'You should have told me the moment you saw me.'

Harriet said nothing, reflecting wryly that the chance would have been a fine thing. He had hardly given her a chance to get a word in edgeways, he had been much too busy grumbling about Felix!

'Here.' She passed him the piece of paper with the name and address of the family written on it. 'You'll need this.'

Philippe glanced briefly at it, slammed the jeep in gear, and started off down the mountain road towards the town of Bodrum.

As they went down through the dark countryside, negotiating a series of hairpin bends, Harriet saw a gipsy encampment. From the light of the Calor gas lamps and the large camp fire, she could see that the tents were made of a patchwork of goatskins. A large number of goats and camels were tethered together within the enclave of the camp. It looked beautiful, like a scene from a biblical film, but Harriet knew life in the camp must be harsh. She wondered if the gipsy women of that morning had come from there.

It didn't take long to reach Bodrum, and soon the jeep was bumping along through narrow cobbled streets, as they looked for the address on the paper. Philippe knew more or less where it was. When they reached the far side of town—the poorest area—the alleyways were too narrow for the jeep to get through, so they left it and walked. They found the house where the family lived. It comprised just two rooms, one up and one down, with a little outhouse at the back where all the cooking and washing were done.

Although she'd been adamant that she could

NEW BEGINNINGS

manage alone, when they actually arrived, Harriet was glad Philippe was with her. It meant there were no language problems. The entire family, except for the sick child, was in the downstairs room busily making shoes. The father was cutting the soles from an enormous hide of leather, the children applying glue to the uppers, and the mother was stitching whole shoes together. Harriet noticed the ancient sewing machine she was using; it looked more appropriate for the Victoria and Albert Museum than for everyday use.

'Tomorrow morning they will sell these on a stall in the Kale Cad market,' said Philippe, 'and tomorrow night they will make more.'

'It must be a very hard life,' observed Harriet.

Philippe's face softened. 'It is,' he agreed. 'This is their only source of income, and they must make enough money from the tourists in summer to last them through the winter.'

'And do they?' asked Harriet.

'Sometimes; if not, their family usually helps out. But, as you noticed, it is a hard life. The tourists come and go, and all they ever see is blue sea, sun and the mountains. They never look beyond, at the people themselves.'

'I'm sure some do,' said Harriet. 'I would.'

Philippe turned and flashed her a sudden smile that sent her heart slamming against her ribcage, making her feel breathless. 'I know you would,' he said.

Although their livelihood depended on it, all shoemaking stopped as soon as Harriet and Philippe stepped inside. The young mother swept the table clear of the mountain of equipment, and rushed outside to begin making coffee.

'Oh, please tell her not to bother,' said Harriet, horrified at putting a stop to the cottage industry.

'They will be very offended if we don't take a thimbleful of coffee,' said Philippe, 'it would be considered most impolite.'

'In that case, of course, I must accept,' said Harriet quickly, indicating in sign language that she would love some coffee. Her reward was beaming smiles all round.

'We'll go upstairs while waiting for the coffee,' said Philippe.

Harriet followed, climbing the narrow stairs to the little room where all the children slept together. It was spartan in its furnishings, but spotlessly clean. There were no beds, but piles of rugs for each child, and on one of these lay the small boy Harriet had seen that morning.

'Good,' she said to Philippe, 'the mother has done exactly as I asked, and propped him up with rugs and pillows so that he is not lying flat.'

'Of course,' said Philippe, sounding slightly surprised. 'Did you expect less?'

'English mothers aren't always so sensible.'

'English mothers are too used to having

hospitals and doctors do everything for them,' commented Philippe.

Harriet couldn't disagree. 'Yes, familiarity sometimes breeds contempt,' she said.

She noted, too, that a glass and jug of water were close by, and that the boy's face was not quite as flushed as it had been in the morning.

Philippe examined him and took his temperature. Then he called down the stairs to the mother. 'I'm asking if he has had his evening dose of syrup,' he explained to Harriet.

An answer came back up, and Philippe nodded. 'The answer is not yet.' He opened the doctor's bag he had brought with him. 'I'll give him an injection now instead. Might as well get the next dose of antibiotic into the system as quickly as possible.'

Without waiting to be asked, Harriet rolled the pyjama sleeve up the small arm, and gently swabbed an area with an alcohol-impregnated tissue. Then Philippe gave the injection, chatting to his small patient as he did so. Harriet listened to his gentle voice, and watched his sensitive hands slide the needle in so quickly and skilfully that the child didn't even notice. You certainly know how to switch on the bedside manner, she thought, no one could resist you! Of course, most doctors were adept at turning on the charm, even Felix had that ability, but his charm wasn't anywhere near as potent as Philippe's.

When it was finished, Harriet rolled the

pyjama sleeve back into place. '*Nasilsiniz?*' she asked in halting Turkish.

'*Iyiyim,*' the small boy replied with a shy smile.

Philippe looked at her thoughtfully. 'I didn't know you had progressed to actually speaking Turkish.'

'I can't,' admitted Harriet ruefully, 'not really. Just a few phrases like "how are you", "*nasilsiniz*", hello, goodbye, thank you—the usual things. But I have tried to learn things that will be useful to me in my work.'

'So I can see,' said Philippe. 'And what did he answer?'

'He said, "very well",' said Harriet triumphantly, glad that her persistence with the phrase book and dictionary were paying off.

'I'm most impressed, Miss Jones,' said Philippe, raising his dark eyebrows and smiling broadly. 'You will soon be speaking Turkish like a native, and I shall want to keep you here.'

Harriet smiled back shyly, her cheeks flooding with colour at the unexpected compliment. Then she hurriedly busied herself repacking his bag, in an attempt to hide the blush.

Philippe Krir was an enigma to her, but he touched a raw chord in her emotions. He was strong and dominant, and yet at the same time she sensed he was vulnerable, as he had been earlier that evening when he had been confiding his doubts about Felix. She knew that he had wanted her assurance that he was right in his

NEW BEGINNINGS

approach, and that Felix was wrong. But, chaotic and confused as her emotions were, Harriet knew that slowly but surely she was falling in love with Philippe. He had woven a spell about her, and she was powerless to prevent herself being drawn to his charismatic personality.

The small boy was now in his arms, and he was teasing him. Harriet slid a sideways glance, and studied his profile overtly. It was imperious, that was the only word that could possibly describe it. Imperious and dominating, she mused, and yet gentle. Then suddenly the memory of the previous night's kiss leaped vividly into her mind, and she knew that whatever Philippe thought of her, she couldn't possibly marry Felix. She didn't love him. It was very simple, really, marriage was unthinkable.

It was sad, but only a little bit! The worst part would be telling Felix. Harriet sighed. How on earth should she broach that?

'That was a sad sigh.' Suddenly she realised that Philippe had put the little boy back to bed, and tucked him up. Now he was standing watching her. 'You look as if you've got the troubles of the world on your shoulders.' He said gently, 'Want to share them?'

'No,' said Harriet much too quickly, then added, 'I mean, I don't have any troubles to share.' She attempted a light-hearted laugh, which was a mistake because it came out as a strangled squeak. 'What ever gave you that idea?'

Philippe was silent for a moment, then shrugged his shoulders. 'I tend to jump to conclusions,' he said abruptly. 'It's a bad habit.'

Harriet followed him down the stairs. The table had been cleared and laid ready. The husband drew up a chair for Harriet, and another for Philippe, then the family sat down. Everyone except the mother, Harriet noticed. She was too busy pouring coffee into tiny cups of gold and blue porcelain. On the table were ornately worked brass trays, filled with a variety of little cakes covered in honey and pistachio nuts.

The coffee was strong and bitter and the cakes very sweet. Harriet didn't really like either, but, because the family was watching her avidly, she managed two cups of coffee and two cakes. Philippe did all the talking, and at last to her relief he stood up to go. Taking her cue from him, she also rose to her feet. When they got to the door, the family shook hands ceremoniously.

'*Allahaismarladik.*' Harriet hoped she had remembered the word for goodbye correctly.

Grins and bobbing heads, and the chorus of '*Gule gule,*' answered her. Harriet felt triumphant: she had got it right.

Philippe led the way back down the narrow street to where the jeep was parked. He opened the door and Harriet climbed in.

NEW BEGINNINGS

'Now,' he said, getting in beside her, and turning to her in the darkness. 'Where shall I take you? Where would you like to go?'

He seemed very large, and overpoweringly close in the confines of the jeep. The faint but recognisable musky fragrance of sandalwood permeated the air. It reminded Harriet of the way his skin had felt beneath her fingertips the night before, dry and warm. A sudden flood of panic washed over her. This man stirred her senses in a way no other man had ever done. Every fibre of her being longed to reach out and touch him.

'Well? Where to?' He leaned towards her. 'You haven't answered my question.'

'Where to?' Her throat felt as if it was encased in iron. 'Back to the hospital, of course.' Amazingly, she heard her voice speaking as if from far away, as if someone else was doing the talking. She sounded cool and composed, the very reverse of how she was actually feeling.

'I'm not taking you back there. You're off duty. Think of something else. You stayed behind last night, so you are going out tonight.' With that decisive pronouncement, Philippe dismissed her words and started the engine. The jeep began to roll forward.

'I don't know where to suggest,' said Harriet, realising he had no intention of taking her back. 'What do you think?'

'I think we should go to Torba, my village,' he

said firmly, not giving her time to argue. 'There is a beautiful taverna right by the harbour. We can sit and have a leisurely drink, and get to know each other better. And,' he added on a teasing note, 'I'm sure you'd like to wash away some of that strong Turkish coffee. You were valiant, drinking two cups.'

'I liked it.' Harriet lied hastily. 'But a visit to Torba would be nice.'

She was curious, too, to see what sort of place he had chosen to live in. Quite apart from the fact that there was no alternative but to accept his invitation gracefully. If it could be called an invitation—it was more like a hijacking! She felt a little perturbed at his remark about getting to know each other better. Half of her longed to find out everything there was to know about him, but the other half was wary. Plus the fact that there was only so much that she dared let him find out about her! She wished she'd already had a chance to tell Felix she wasn't going to marry him. The guilty secret of their engagement hung around her neck like a leaden weight.

She sat in silence as he manoeuvred the jeep through the narrow streets, and out of the town. Then they began to climb up a steeply winding road, the headlights illuminating great bare slabs of granite as they twisted and turned through the road cut through mountains. Philippe was silent too and, when Harriet slid him a sideways glance, appeared to be wholly concentrating on the road.

After about twenty minutes the road started descending, and eventually the jeep emerged from the granite cuttings into an enclosed bay.

The outlines of the high mountains surrounding the dark mass of sea stood out in sharp black relief against the navy blue of the night sky. Here and there, clusters of lights along the shoreline indicated the presence of small villages; but high up in the mountains there was nothing, not even the occasional pinprick of light. All was darkness.

'All olives and figs,' said Philippe, waving towards the blackness of the mountains. 'I must bring you here in the daytime. It's very wild, but also very beautiful.'

'From what little I've seen, most of Turkey is very wild and beautiful. Quite different from southern England where I come from,' said Harriet. 'But of course you must know that. Didn't you spend most of your childhood in England? I seem to remember either Laila or Halide saying so.'

Philippe laughed, but it was a bitter sound. 'There is not much you can teach me about England,' he agreed. 'As a child I spent a great deal of my life there. My father was a dedicated anglophile, more English than the English. I didn't even know I was half Turkish until I went to school. But since I qualified in medicine, I've lived here. Unlike my father, I am not ashamed of the land of my birth. I belong here.'

'Yes, you do,' agreed Harriet, 'you suit the

place.' The last words came out in a rush as the jeep suddenly jolted to an abrupt halt.

Philippe had stopped beside a low whitewashed building, fronted by a terrace with a tiled roof. The side of the terrace had minaret-shaped arches which opened directly on to the low harbour wall. Flickering lights on the walls and tables were reflected in the inky blackness of the sea immediately below the building.

Philippe leapt out of the driving seat and came round to help Harriet down. 'And what do you mean by that remark?' he queried softly. 'You suit the place!'

'Well . . . I mean, you look like a Turk,' said Harriet, without thinking.

'And what exactly does a Turk look like?'

Although his voice was soft and low, Harriet felt a prickling of dismay crawl along her spine. She had offended him with her thoughtless words; perhaps he thought she meant it in a derogatory sense.

'I mean that . . .' she stopped, and looked up at him.

How large he seemed looming above her in the darkness. How could she put into the right words what she really meant? It would sound silly to say that he blended in perfectly with his surroundings, whether it was in the opulence of the palace, a primitive little town house, or the beautiful untamed countryside; he belonged to all those places. That a thousand years of history were written across the planes and angles of his bronzed face. Greek, Persian, Ottoman, all those ancient civilisations had combined to make the man who stood before her now. A proud, imperious Turkish doctor, who cared for his country and his people with a deep and committed passion. Harriet instinctively realised that part of his pride stemmed from the fact that his father had been ashamed of being Turkish.

Philippe interrupted her rambling thoughts impatiently. 'I suppose you like Nordic types. Someone like Felix Hamilton-Wirrell.' He laughed caustically. 'Hamilton-Wirrell, what a ridiculous name! Why can't he call himself either Hamilton or Wirrell?'

'It is not ridiculous,' said Harriet. She felt duty-bound to stick up for Felix. 'You know as well as I do that double-barrelled names are quite common. And yes, I do like Felix, not because he's Nordic, as you put it, but because——' She'd been about to say, because he's a good doctor, but Philippe interrupted her before she could get the words out.

'Because you are engaged to be married to him.'

The remark was fired at her, without warning, and with the deadly accuracy of a high velocity bullet.

'How did you know?' She gasped; startled and slightly frightened by his tone of voice. Involuntarily she took a step backwards. In the darkness she missed her footing and stumbled on the unmade road.

Philippe reached out to catch her, but Harriet, already unnerved by his remark, didn't feel up to coping with an action replay of the previous night, and stubbornly moved away. However, more off balance than she'd thought, she felt herself falling. It took a split second for the full horror to register. Then she realised she was not falling on to the road, but hurtling instead over the edge of the path, heading straight for the waters of the harbour.

The inky water closed above her head and she came up spluttering and coughing. Shaking the wet hair out of her eyes like a spaniel, she trod water vigorously. The water was freezing. I might as well be in the Arctic, she thought, furious at her own stupidity.

'Ahoy, there!'

Looking up, she could see Philippe's head as he looked over the edge, and to her vexation he was laughing. 'I want to get out,' she said, and sneezed.

'Fate is punishing you for lying to me about your engagement!' he said, making no effort to help her.

'I did not lie,' shouted Harriet, trying to stop her teeth from chattering. 'You never asked me!' She looked around for some steps to climb up out of the water, but in the darkness none was visible. 'Are you going to help me get out, or are you going to let me drown?' she demanded.

'I'm thinking about it,' came the reply, 'and I think maybe I *should* let you drown!' Then a long arm came down and he leaned over the edge. Grasping her outstretched hand in his, he hauled her out like a lobster pot from the harbour waters, and unceremoniously dumped her back on the path.

A riot of conflicting emotions raced through Harriet's head as she stood dripping and cold on the pathway. Anger because he had obviously known about the engagement for some time, and had not said a damned thing, instead sneakily waiting for her to fall into a trap. And fury at herself for falling into the trap he'd set so neatly, and then, to cap it all, into the harbour!

'You'll have to take me back,' she said crossly, trying in vain to wring some of the sea-water from the hem of her dress. 'I can't go for a drink now.'

'I had already decided I didn't want to take such a dishonest woman for a drink.'

'I am *not* dishonest, I——' Harriet turned towards him raising her hands in an expression of denial.

Whether he caught her outstretched hands, or whether she put her arms around him, she didn't know. But somehow she was in his arms, and his face was inches from hers. In a voice that sounded thick and rough, he said just two words. 'Kiss me.'

Without stopping to think, Harriet obeyed. It was an obedience born of her own desire and Philippe's command. His strong hands slid to span her waist, long dark fingers imprisoning her slender body. Not that Harriet felt like a prisoner, because not for one moment did it occur to her to resist. There was something verging on the hypnotic about the way his mouth captured hers. As if, by taking her lips, he had in some mysterious way perfected complete control over her whole body. With a sigh she parted her lips to his invading tongue, and let her mind drift aimlessly on an intoxicating tide of surging emotions. I'm drowning, she thought dreamily, but I don't care.

CHAPTER SIX

BUT even the fiercest passion couldn't keep the cold at bay for ever. The icy sea-water eventually penetrated through to her bones, and Harriet started to shiver violently. Her trembling communicated itself to Philippe, and he drew back. Harriet could tell from the expression on his face that she wasn't the only one who had forgotten she was drenched with salt water.

'I'm wet!' she stammered unnecessarily.

Alternately hot and cold, shivering and blushing at the same time, Harriet thought wryly that she must have just uttered the understatement of the year! Wet — drowned, more likely! Sea-water had soaked through every stitch of clothing, and was running in great rivulets down her body. It streamed from her clothes, her hair, in fact from every conceivable part of her, and was making a fairly large puddle in the dusty road.

'You will get pneumonia,' Philippe said abruptly, using his doctor's voice. 'Come on.'

With one swift movement, and before she had a chance to demur, he swung her up into his arms, carrying her as if she weighed no more than a feather. Striding past the taverna, he continued on towards a large villa, set a little way from the sea. From the cradle of his arms, Harriet could see the villa was surrounded by tall, dark cypress trees. It was a huge building, and in the darkness the trees gave it an air of isolation. Surely that enormous house couldn't be where he lived?

'Where are we going?' Harriet struggled ineffectually, trying to put her feet to the ground. 'Put me down,' she insisted. 'I can walk by myself.'

Philippe seemed not to notice her struggles, and took not the slightest notice of what she said. 'To my home,' he said briefly as if she hadn't spoken, and continued walking towards the villa.

'To your home! Oh, but I don't think——'

'Stop thinking,' rapped the uncompromising reply, 'because that is where we are going, and no arguments!'

Harriet's heart changed gear, and started thudding wildly out of control. To his home, with Philippe—alone! She'd already kissed him twice, with what could only be described as wanton abandon. Much against my better judgement, she reminded herself quickly, if somewhat weakly! Now, she knew she just *had* to say no. Now was not the time to be weak-willed again; because, once inside, and alone with Philippe, Harriet knew she couldn't possibly answer for her actions, the attraction between them was too strong. It was now or never!

'Philippe,' she began, trying to keep her voice firm and determined. 'You now that I'm engaged to Felix. So you know why I really shouldn't have kissed you.'

For the moment, Harriet had decided, it would be more convenient to stay engaged to Felix. The thought that she loved another man should appeal to Philippe's conscience!

'No, you really shouldn't have,' he said euphemistically, his tone ringing with wry accusation. 'If you were engaged to me, I'd wring your neck if you went around kissing other men!'

'But you kissed me first,' flared Harriet indignantly. Oh, dear, perhaps it wasn't such a good idea pretending to still be engaged. Now he thought she was some hard-hearted hussy, only too willing to have a fling with whoever was available! 'I was taken by surprise,' she continued, still sounding indignant. 'On both occasions,' she added for good measure.

'Agreed,' Philippe said. 'But don't pile all the blame on me. I was taken by surprise myself. It was not something I had intended to do. But I am only an ordinary man, and the physical temptation of a very beautiful woman in my arms was too strong.'

'Beautiful?' whispered Harriet in surprise.

Felix had never told her she was beautiful, and she'd got used to thinking he was the handsome one of the twosome.

Philippe stopped walking for a moment, and stood still, looking down at her in the dim light. A smile curved his stern lips as he said softly, 'Yes, beautiful.' Then he added, 'But to get back to the point, my dear Harriet, I can't say that I noticed you putting up very much resistance, even if I did make the first move!'

'No,' agreed Harriet, in a subdued whisper, 'I didn't, and that is why I mustn't go with you to your villa. My resistance is low, at least, it seems to be where you are concerned. I think I ought to go back to the hospital now.' Her voice broke with pleading. 'Please, Philippe.'

To her rising consternation, Philippe's only reply was to give a husky chuckle, and say, 'Isn't there a song called "My Resistance is Low"?'

He strode forward again, and they reached the garden of the villa. A cloud of white jasmine hung in a mist of starry flowers over the gateway, and great wafts of the delicate fragrance enveloped them as they passed by. When they reached the white marble steps leading up to the arched entrance before the main door, Philippe at last put Harriet down on to her feet.

Then, with a rueful laugh, he spun her round to face him. 'Don't worry too much about your lack of resistance, or mine either for that matter,' he said wryly. 'My mother will take care of things!'

'Your mother?'

'Yes, she is staying with me, while her own villa is being completed. It's being built over there.' He pointed to the opposite side of the bay. 'So you see, you have nothing to fear from me, or yourself,' he added casually as an afterthought.

He fished for a key in his pocket, and Harriet slid him a sideways glance. The crisp darkness of his hair shone in the light of the porch lamp. It was as much as she could do to stop herself from reaching to touch it, and she couldn't make up her mind whether she was pleased, or sorry, that they were not to be alone. One half of her subconscious heaved an enormous sigh of relief; at least she wouldn't have to put her will-power, or lack of it, to the test! But the other half, the more contrary half, wondered what might have happened if they *had* been alone!

'Oh, well, in that case I'll agree to come in,' she heard herself saying airily.

'I wasn't aware that you had a choice, because I've no intention of taking you back yet!'

Harriet began to feel annoyed. Why was it he always seemed to have the upper hand? 'If I really wanted to, I'd walk back,' she said crossly.

'It's a damned long way.'

'But not too damned long!'

'Be careful, Harriet. Or you might find yourself

regretting those words,' Philippe replied drily. 'I could call your bluff!'

'It's not bluff,' muttered Harriet, shivering violently and wishing he'd hurry up and open the door. All the same, she decided it might be prudent to remain quiet, at least until she'd had a chance to dry herself!

At last, the heavy wooden door, studded with shining brass studs, swung open, and Philippe ushered a shivering Harriet into a cool and elegant hallway. Black and white tiles on the floor threw the plain white walls, hung with expensive tapestries, into stark relief. A shining marble stairway curved around the hall upwards and out of sight, and several wide archways led off into other parts of the ground floor of the villa.

Apart from the tapestries, the only ornaments were amphorae spilling over with trailing fronds of green fern. These were supported in wrought iron frames, and were placed at artistic intervals around the hall. Harriet could see at a glance that they were ancient, and had obviously been retrieved from the sea bed; the remains of tiny crustaceans were clearly visible on the ancient pottery of the wine jars.

The uncluttered elegance of the surroundings did nothing to restore her nervous apprehension, or the already low ebb of her self-confidence. Streams of muddy water dripped with monotonous regularity from the hem of her sodden dress, steadily creeping like the tide over the previously pristinely clean floor.

'Mother,' called Philippe.

A doorway under one of the arches opened briskly, and a tall, dark woman glided into the centre of the entrance hall. She was beautiful, and exquisitely well-groomed from each shining hair on her head down to her pearly fingernails. Harriet shuffled awkwardly in her muddy puddle, knowing she looked like something the cat had dragged in.

'Mother,' said Philippe, firmly propelling a very reluctant Harriet forward, 'may I introduce you to Harriet Jones? One of my English nurses.'

'How nice to meet you, my dear. I've been wondering what Philippe's new nurses were like.'

Harriet grasped the smoothly manicured hand with her own cold and muddy one. But Philippe's mother smiled with genuine warmth, and her eyes, the same strange colour as her son's, reflected the smile. Her tone of voice was friendly and matter-of-fact, and she made Harriet feel as if she was introduced to dripping wet girls every day of the week.

Even so, Harriet wished the floor would open and swallow her up. She hadn't felt so embarrassed since she had been a student, and had fallen into a bath with one of the patients!

Hastily murmuring a greeting in reply, she

added apologetically, 'I'm terribly sorry about all the water on the floor. I'm afraid I fell into the harbour.'

Madame Krir gave a gentle laugh. 'Oh, dear! Well, so long as it was a fall and my son didn't push you!' She saw the puzzled expression flicker across Harriet's face and hastened to explain. 'He pushed Fatima once, into that very same harbour, when they were having one of their violent arguments.'

'Mother!' Philippe sounded annoyed, but the affection in his eyes belied his voice. 'That was years and years ago, when we were teenagers. And anyway, she did fall.'

'I can only repeat what Fatima told me, my dear,' said his mother firmly, ignoring his protestations. 'Now, Harriet, come upstairs,' she beckoned Harriet to follow her, 'we must get you out of those wet things and find you some dry clothes.'

Madame Krir stayed with her while she showered and changed. She was obviously pleased to have another female to talk to. Although Harriet missed a good fifty per cent of the conversation because of the noise of the shower, she did find out that although Fatima lived in Istanbul most of the year, when she came to the south she usually stayed at Philippe's villa.

'I think you and Fatima are about the same size,' said Madame Krir, rifling through a large wardrobe packed with clothes as Harriet emerged from the shower. 'I'm afraid there are only Turkish clothes here. It's one of Fatima's indulgences. She says they make her feel more comfortable, and she likes to relax when she gets away from the city.'

'Oh . . . well, perhaps mine could be dried——' began Harriet, wondering why Fatima needed to relax, and how often she stayed with Philippe.

'You don't mind, do you? Wearing these I mean?' Madame Krir held up a pile of rich-looking silk material.

'Oh, no,' said Harriet hastily, 'but Fatima might.'

'Good heavens, no! She has so many clothes, and she never wears half of them.'

'What does Fatima do in Istanbul?' Harriet asked, curiosity getting the better of her.

Madame Krir was more than eager to talk. 'She runs an import-export business. Originally she was in partnership with her husband, but since his accident she has run it alone, and very successfully, too. She travels the world a great deal, it's lucky she's fluent in Arabic, French and English.' She laughed softly. 'I would never have believed it possible a few years ago, but now she is a woman working in a man's world, and beating them at their own game.'

'She sounds very clever,' said Harriet, feeling totally inadequate in comparison.

'She is,' said Madame Krir, 'and an example to

all women. When her husband was killed three years ago, she could have easily gone into mourning, and then just waited to remarry. But no, she has proved she can stand on her own two feet.'

'I expect she will remarry one day,' said Harriet carefully.

'Of course.' Madame Krir gave a self-conscious laugh. 'Actually I have a few plans up my sleeve in that respect.' She looked at Harriet. 'But you won't mention that to Fatima, will you? Or Philippe,' she added as an afterthought.

'I wouldn't dream of it,' said Harriet unhappily.

When she was ready, Philippe's mother led the way back downstairs, and a dried and perfumed Harriet followed shyly. The dark green, voluminous trousers emphasised her slender figure, and the hand-printed silk shirt, in a paler shade of green, clung to the outline of her rounded breasts.

'I feel like something out of Scheherazade,' she said self-consciously.

Madame Krir laughed. 'It suits you. I'm sure Philippe will approve.'

Harriet followed her through a large airy room at the back of the villa, into another which opened out on to a terrace leading into the garden. The air was bursting with the sounds and perfumes of the night. And, although she couldn't see it, Harriet knew there must be a pool, because she could hear the throaty croaking of frogs mingling among the other night sounds, and now and then there was the faint splash of a fish as it leaped to catch an unwary insect.

'You like the pot-pourri of perfumes from my garden?' Philippe came on to the terrace, carrying a silver salver on which stood a bottle of red wine and three glasses.

Harriet drew a deep breath, drinking in the sweetness of the air. 'Yes,' she said truthfully. As she spoke, the sweet notes of a nightingale fell like a waterfall of sound into the night.

Philippe's mother drew Harriet forward from where she was standing in the shadow at the edge of the terrace. 'There,' she said to Philippe, once Harriet was in the light. 'Your English nurse is transformed into a Turkish girl.'

The gold of his eyes blazed for a moment with amber fire, then was masked as he remarked wryly, 'The perfect outfit for the seraglio!'

Although he had hardly glanced at her, Harriet knew that the fleeting glance he had shot in her direction had registered every single detail.

'I . . . I'm a little larger than Fatima,' she muttered, wishing that quite so much of her cleavage wasn't visible.

'I noticed!' was his only comment.

But his lips curved in an appreciative, if slightly mocking smile as he spoke. He was laughing at her because she was dressed in a similar manner to a woman of the ancient seraglio, and he knew how she felt about that!

'Perfect for the seraglio? Philippe, what do you mean?' The voice of Philippe's mother cut across their conversation.

'That is where we live. Myself and the other girls,' said Harriet quickly, glad of the interruption. 'I'm afraid I was rather rude to Philippe about being given such accommodation.'

'You said it was a prison, if I remember correctly,' said Philippe, watching her, a challenge in the gold of his eyes. He poured out three glasses of wine.

Harriet responded to the challenge. 'It *was* a prison once. Oh, I know it was many years ago, but you can't deny it all the same. No matter what fancy name you like to call it,' said Harriet heatedly. She turned away from the amusement in Philippe's eyes, and back towards his mother. 'But I've got used to it now. In fact,' she heard herself confessing to Madame Krir, 'I love the peace and tranquillity of the place. It's so different from my flat in London, which had a never-ending stream of traffic roaring past the windows.'

Philippe pulled up three wickerwork chairs, deeply upholstered in pale leather, and the three of them sat down. Harriet accepted a glass of wine, and sank back into the comfortable depths of the chair.

Philippe held up his glass of wine to the lamp, twisting it so that the light shone through the angles of the cut glass, shooting out sparks of brilliant ruby red.

'Enjoy this,' he said to Harriet. 'It is made by a brave family in Lebanon, in the Bekaa valley. Against all odds, and in spite of the civil war, Château Musar continues to be produced.'

'Don't change the subject, Philippe,' said his mother sharply, determined not to be sidetracked. 'Why on earth did you put the girls in the seraglio of all places? That wasn't very tactful. There are plenty of other empty wings in the palace.'

'Ah, but none so beautiful, or *appropriate*,' he said, giving the last word a wickedly provocative note.

Harriet shot him a frosty glance, but decided not to rise to the bait. He really was the most infuriating man. A moment ago she was melting in his arms, and now she was melting with bottled-up annoyance, and he knew it! She sat in silence, sipping the wine with its distinctive spiced, smoky taste.

'Does Fatima know?' Madame Krir sounded slightly exasperated.

'Not yet, I haven't had much time to take to her.' Philippe, too, sipped his wine, then he added reflectively, 'Anyway, somehow I don't think she'll be particularly interested. Not at the moment.' His voice hardened, and the expression on his face perceptibly darkened. 'Her thoughts seem to be almost solely occupied by a very handsome English surgeon, who is intent on helping her spend her inheritance.'

'Yes, but on an operating table for the hospital,' interrupted Harriet quickly. 'You make it sound as if Felix is after her money for himself.'

'In a way, he is,' said Philippe with a scowl.

Draining his wine glass, he set it down with a bad-tempered crash on the copper table beside him.

'I take it you do not approve of this purchase,' his mother remarked mildly.

'It's unnecessary. Fatima shouldn't waste her money.'

Madame Krir laughed. 'Fatima is a young woman with a strong mind of her own. You, of all people, should know that. She will spend her money on whatever she wishes. And as for wasting it, well . . .' Madame Krir shrugged her shoulders expressively. 'She has so much, she will never spend it all in her lifetime!'

Harriet watched Philippe. His face had taken on the expression of chiselled granite as his mother had talked of Fatima. Miserably Harriet thought she knew why. There was definitely something more than just friendship between Philippe and Fatima.

A sudden rage swept through her, fury at

her own stupidity for allowing herself to become enmeshed in attraction for this man. Taking refuge in her anger, she turned on Philippe fiercely.

'I think I know Felix well enough to say that he would never knowingly waste money,' Harriet said in the most disdainful tone she could muster. 'He thinks your hospital needs a certain type of operating table, and you disagree. It's a professional disagreement between two medical men. You should sort it out together, without getting other people to take sides.'

'I haven't asked your opinion, and yet it sounds to me as if you *are* taking sides. His side!' snapped Philippe. There was a deathly hush as they sat for a moment glaring stonily at one another.

'Tell me, my dear,' Madame Krir interrupted hastily, breaking the awkward silence. 'This man Felix, what is he like? Do you think Fatima is interested in him as a man, or he in her as a woman?'

Harriet swallowed and glared at Philippe, who suddenly looked amused. Damn you, she thought angrily, the flash of insight coming too late, you've manoeuvred me just exactly where you wanted to get me. Into a corner!

'Felix is . . .' She hesitated, then carefully steadied her voice. 'A very attractive Englishman. He is also a dedicated surgeon, and wants to improve the hospital. I'm sure he is not interested in Fatima just because she is a woman, but because she is someone who can help.'

'You mean, you *hope* he's not interested.' The words were low, audible only to Harriet's ears, as Philippe leaned forward to refill her glass.

It was tantamount to waving a red rag to a bull, and Harriet heard herself saying very firmly, 'I hope, for Fatima's sake, that she doesn't fall in love with Felix, because she will only end up being unhappy.'

'You know this Felix very well?' Philippe's mother eyed her astutely, and Harriet realised that perhaps she had been a little too adamant in her statement.

'We've worked closely together for over three years,' she said, quickly, but choosing her words with care, 'and in all that time, I have never known him easily deflected from his chosen course. It's common knowledge that he aims to be a world-famous surgeon, and I think he will succeed, because he is intensely ambitious. Everything else takes second place in his life.'

'Spoken like a true and faithful little fi . . . friend and colleague,' commented Philippe wryly.

Harriet frowned at him. She was certain he'd been about to say the world 'fiancée, but for some reason had stopped.

'Felix sounds almost too ambitious.' Harriet turned her attention back to Madame Krir as she spoke. 'I'm not sure that's always a good thing.' She placed her empty glass on the salver and stood to go. 'You must make sure poor Fatima does not get her heart broken,' she said to her son. 'Pay her more attention, the poor child has suffered enough. Try and spend more time with her.'

'I fully intend to,' said Philippe firmly, as he rose too. He kissed his mother goodnight.

It seemed to Harriet the height of cynicism. He intended to pay court to Fatima, but wasn't averse to a little dalliance on the side! How chauvinistic could a man get! After politely bidding Madame Krir goodnight, Harriet could hardly wait for her to get out of hearing. The second she was sure it was safe to speak, she leaped to her feet.

'I think you're quite despicable,' she said.

'What are you on about? I've never known a girl as unpredictable as you,' came the lazy response as he poured himself some more wine.

'You know perfectly well what I'm talking about,' said Harriet vehemently, wondering how he could remain so cool.

Restlessly she moved across to the edge of the terrace, and looked out into the darkness of the garden. I ought to be going now, she thought. Then sensed rather than heard Philippe move and come to stand behind her. Every fibre of her being tingled into awareness at his presence. Go away, she wanted to shout, but her mouth was dry, and the unspoken words lodged like stones in her throat.

Philippe's fingers softly caressed her bare arm. 'Felix shouldn't neglect you,' he said, in a voice so low she had to strain her ears to hear him. 'I want you, Harriet, and I know you want me.' I really ought not to, thought Harriet as slowly he turned her unresisting body to face him and put his arms about her. 'You are everything a woman should be. Soft, pliant.' He kissed the throbbing hollow of her throat. 'Eager to know, and to be known.'

'Philippe, I . . .' The words trailed away in a gasp as Philippe pushed aside her shirt-top, and his lips gently slid along her bare shoulder. It felt so wonderful, it would have been a sacrilege to waste time talking.

Everything merged into a hazy blur as his hard body closed around her soft one. Arms like iron bands pinned her close against the solid warmth of his body and his mouth moved upwards, burning a tingling pathway towards her lips. As his mouth finally closed over hers, Harriet was conscious of nothing but the whirlpool of sensual longing that engulfed her in shivering waves. Involuntarily her arms slid up around his neck, pulling his dark head closer, and she gave herself up to the primeval desire of a woman wanting to be mastered. She wanted nothing more at that moment than to belong to Philippe, the man whose hands had the touch of fiery velvet, and whose mouth was now teaching her ways of kissing she had never known existed.

He lifted his head and looked at her, amber eyes glittering with raw desire, a dark line of colour on his cheekbones. Harriet gazed back, face flushed, her green eyes smoky with sensuality. 'Yes, Felix can have his damned operating table.' He laughed, a throaty triumphant sound. 'I've got you in return.'

Harriet felt as if she had just taken a cold shower, only instead of water she had been showered with daggers of ice. 'Why you . . . you . . .' She stumbled over her words. 'I wouldn't be so attractive if I didn't belong to Felix, would I? You really are despicable!' With a mighty effort, she pushed hard on his chest and succeeded in disentangling herself from his embrace.

'Don't be so ridiculous,' said Philippe sharply. 'Anyway, I've proved to both of us that you don't love Felix. Why did you ever get engaged at all? It's a sham!'

'I do love Felix. It wasn't, it isn't—oh . . .' Words failed her. Without thinking Harriet lashed out in mingled pain and fury, and her hand came down with stinging force across Philippe's cheek. A raw weal formed on his dark skin, the perfect imprint of her fingers. 'Take me back to my room at the hospital, *now*,' she half shouted, half sobbed.

'I'll take you back, you little wild cat.' Philippe

was furiously angry too, the livid mark of her fingers flared into prominence as the light caught his face. Grabbing her arms, he held them rigidly to her side, so tightly that Harriet gasped with pain. 'I'll take you back, and throw you in the seraglio where you belong. You've slapped my face once too often.'

'What have you in mind when we get there? Are you going to force me to submit?' jeered Harriet, throwing caution and tact to the winds. 'I suppose that's your style, after all, you are half——'

For a moment the rage on Philippe's face was so great that she thought he would knock her to the ground. 'Half Turkish?' he grated harshly, adding, 'And while you're about it, why don't you say half civilised?'

Too late, Harriet realised she'd overstepped the mark. 'I didn't mean——' she began.

A cold, inscrutable blanket settled across Philippe's face—he turned away abruptly. 'You have nothing to fear from me,' he said quietly.

Picking up a bell from the copper table, he rang it twice. The door opened and a man came in. Philippe spoke to him rapidly in Turkish, and then started to walk away down the steps of the terrace into the garden. At the bottom step he turned and looked at Harriet. Even the darkness of the night couldn't disguise the coldness in his eyes. 'Mehmet will drive you back to the hospital,' he said.

'Philippe, I didn't mean . . .' began Harriet again, but it was too late, he had gone. Whatever their differences, Harriet felt indescribably sad, knowing she should never have flung such a terrible insult at him. It was unforgivable. Slowly she followed a slightly puzzled looking Mehmet out through the villa to the jeep.

It was a very subdued Harriet who lay on her bed that night. Even the cooing of a pair of doves who had taken up residence on one of the window-sills failed to soothe her jangled nerves. Miserable, confused and unhappy, she tossed and turned all night. It was not until the first rosy fingers of dawn began to creep into the room that she fell into a restless sleep.

CHAPTER SEVEN

THE arrival the following morning, a week earlier than expected, of the other English nurse, Janet Price, prevented Harriet from brooding too much over the misunderstanding with Philippe.

Janet, a flaming redhead and oozing self-confidence, breezed in. 'I've travelled all the way from Dalaman to Bodrum by taxi,' she announced cheerfully.

Harriet gave a mental shudder. 'Good heavens, that must have cost a fortune!'

Janet laughed. 'It's only money,' she said, 'and I wanted to see this hospital I've heard so much about. Give me a few hours' sleep, and I'll be ready for work.'

It was easy to take an immediate liking to her, and Harriet gave her a brief tour of the hospital as there was no sign of Philippe.

'When will he be here?' Janet wanted to know.

'I don't know,' said Harriet truthfully, wishing she did. The sooner she could get her apology over and done with, the better!

They were in the intensive care unit, and Harriet was telling Janet the dramatic saga of their very first case, the stabbing, when Sofi came hurrying in with a note.

'Oh, hell,' groaned Harriet on reading it.

'Problems?'

'Yes, Suzy's gone down with a bug.'

'Never mind, I'm here now,' said Janet. 'I told you I don't need much rest. Put me to work.'

Harriet made up her mind quickly. 'OK, I'll install you in your room and start my clinic. Then perhaps you could sort out our post-op patients this afternoon.'

'Good as done,' said Janet cheerfully, following Harriet as she hurried down the corridor leading to the seraglio.

Like Suzy, Janet was over the moon when she saw the luxury the nurses lived in, and didn't care two hoots about the fact that it had previously been a harem.

'Being a concubine can't possibly be any worse than being a nurse,' she informed Harriet pragmatically.

There was no time to stop and chat, so Harriet left her to recover from the journey, while she set about organising the clinic with Halide. Engrossed in the work, and with still no sign of Barry, there was precious little time to worry about personal problems. The morning flew by, and they easily finished by lunchtime.

'Are we more efficient? Or were there fewer patients?' Harriet looked at her schedule, slightly puzzled.

'Fewer patients,' said Halide abruptly. 'The bus broke down.'

Harriet looked at her in surprise; it was unusual for Halide to sound bad-tempered. But she didn't have time to dwell on it, and leaving her to clear up and prepare for the afternoon session, Harriet dashed along to see Barry. He was still in bed, and terribly apologetic about it.

'But I'm getting up this afternoon,' he said determinedly, when her head popped round the corner of his door, 'even if it kills me!'

'No need for anything as drastic as that,' said Harriet, grinning at Barry's martyred expression, and told him of the arrival of Janet Price.

Barry looked relieved, and slid back down in the bed. 'Hey, what about that sick kid, the one with epiglottitis?'

She told him about the previous night's visit to the sick child in Bodrum.

'Glad to hear Philippe took you,' was his comment. Then he grinned as he teased, 'Did he reward you by showing you the sights of Bodrum afterwards?'

'He took me to Torba, for a drink,' Harriet answered cautiously, omitting to mention her submersion in the harbour, or the fact that she had ended up at Philippe's villa. Somehow, she had more than a suspicion that Philippe wouldn't be mentioning that either!

'I'll definitely be with you tomorrow,' Barry

said as she left. He looked pale, but determined. 'I've got to be. It's the day Philippe wants us to start going out to the more remote villages.'

'Yes, outpatients with a vengeance,' Harriet said. 'I'm looking forward to it.' She had her doubts as to Barry's ability to go trekking around with mobile clinics so soon after his illness, but remained silent. Tomorrow was another day; she'd tackle that when it arrived.

Janet Price reappeared at lunchtime and happily went off to prepare the post-operative patients, so that they were ready to go home when their relatives arrived.

'I hope they'll be able to understand the drug regime they need to follow, and what exercise they're allowed to take,' said Harriet anxiously. 'I wish Philippe was around to give the patients their final check. It's always difficult doing it through an interpreter, and we don't want them back with burst stitches or infection!'

'You worry too much,' Janet said calmly. 'Sofi and I will manage just fine.'

'Sorry!' Harriet grinned. 'I sound like some grumpy old sister tutor! I didn't mean to teach my grandmother to suck eggs! Philippe did say they could go home, but he also said he would be here to look at them. I can't think where he has got to.'

Janet raised her eyebrows. 'What are you worrying about? Philippe must trust your judgement, he wouldn't leave you here alone otherwise.'

'It's a comforting thought, I suppose,' said Harriet, who hadn't thought of it in that light.

Janet was right; whatever Philippe might think about her on a personal level, he must trust her professional judgement. She held that crumb of comfort to her heart, and went along ready to start the afternoon clinic.

She halted at the waiting-room door; it was bursting at the seams with mothers and children. 'Oh dear, half this morning's missing patients seemed to have turned up this afternoon.'

'They have.' Halide sounded distracted, and was rushing round trying to find extra chairs. 'As Ali couldn't pick everyone up this morning, he's brought them now instead.'

Harriet sighed, wishing Ali had postponed some, but there was nothing to be done now, other than to start on the mammoth afternoon clinic.

'He is stupid,' grumbled Halide.

Harriet looked up from scrubbing her hands with Hibiscrub. Halide must have definitely got out of bed the wrong side that morning. 'Oh, well,' she said cheerfully, trying to get Halide to give her a smile, 'let's go into the lions' den.'

But Halide didn't smile back, merely rushed out and brought the first batch of patients in.

NEW BEGINNINGS

The afternoon did not run smoothly. It seemed that, besides having too many patients, they had more than their fair share of noisy, uncooperative children, plus mothers who were not much better. Harriet felt her own patience, usually inexhaustible where children were concerned, beginning to fray at the edges. As for Halide, her temper was definitely more than a little frayed, it was in complete tatters! She snapped back at Harriet, and shouted at the noisy queue of mothers and children outside the treatment cubicle.

Bending over the couch, intent on vaccinating a wriggling child, Harriet didn't notice the sudden and dramatic drop in the noise level at first. When it did register, she merely thought, thank heavens for that, and wondered what Halide had done. The next moment the reason was obvious, the curtains parted and Philippe strode in, looking very displeased.

'Things seem to be a little out of control,' he said abruptly. 'I've sent Halide away.'

Harriet stuck a plaster over the needle entry site on the now quiet child, and looked up. 'Sent Halide away!' She frowned at the tone of censure in his voice. 'A little drastic, surely? It's not her fault that we have a noisy crowd in here today.'

'I didn't say it was her fault,' he said, 'but I'm afraid Halide's mind is on other things.'

'What other things?' Harriet popped a lump of

sugar containing the polio vaccine in the mouth of the small girl she had just vaccinated, and lifting her from the couch sent her on her way.

'Don't you ever talk to your colleagues?' Philippe's voice was cuttingly sarcastic.

'Of course I do.' Harriet glanced up again warily, but his expression was enough for her to hastily avert her gaze.

He was in a blacker than black mood, that was plain enough to see. Now is definitely not the time to bring up the subject of last night, she thought.

'Not enough, evidently,' was his sarcastic comment. 'Otherwise Halide would have told you that her mother went into a diabetic coma late last night. That is where I've been up until now. I've been treating her, and she's on the medical ward now. I've sent Halide along to look after her mother.'

Now he had her full attention, and Harriet clasped a hand to her mouth guiltily. 'I had no idea,' she said, feeling overwhelmed with remorse. 'But is it a good idea for Halide to nurse her? In England we are never allowed to nurse relatives.'

'This is not England,' Philippe rapped back. 'Here, we have no such inhibitions. People want to be involved with those they love. But perhaps you find that difficult to understand!'

Harriet felt hurt at the harshness of his tone.

'I was trained to accept the idea,' she said quietly, 'and I suppose I've never questioned it.'

'A typical Anglo-Saxon reaction,' he snorted.

But Harriet wasn't listening, she was thinking of Halide. She realised with dismay that she ought to have guessed something was wrong, all the signs had been there. 'How could I have been so thoughtless,' she muttered, as much to herself as to Philippe. 'Selfishly engrossed with my own thoughts, I never . . . Oh, poor Halide.'

Philippe's face softened momentarily, then hardened slightly as he said, 'You were worrying about Felix.'

'No I wasn't, I——' Harriet stopped.

She'd been about to blurt out that he, Philippe, had been in her mind more than Felix, and that she bitterly regretted her thoughtless words of the night before. All the things that she wanted to say were poised on her lips, but the stern, unyielding expression on Philippe's face stopped her. The words fluttered on her lips, but died before they had taken life.

'I was preoccupied,' she admitted, adding by way of explanation, 'but it was because Janet Price turned up unexpectedly this morning, and Suzy is sick.' Screwing up her courage she looked directly into his topaz eyes, wanting to apologise, but still something prevented her.

For a moment Philippe regarded her quizzically, his gaze holding hers, then he raised his dark brows in surprise. 'This morning?' he queried.

Harriet nodded, and turning away busied herself quite needlessly tidying the cubicle. It was an effort, acting coolly and naturally as if the previous night had never happened. But somehow she managed it because it seemed to be what Philippe wanted.

'Actually, it turned out to be a blessing in disguise, because Janet has been able to take over Suzy's duties. She's on the surgical ward. Do you want to see her while I carry on here alone?'

Philippe shook his head. 'No need,' he said. 'Janet is a very resourceful girl, she can easily manage on her own. I've never known her not able to cope.'

'You know Janet well?' Harriet tried to squash the blazing surge of plain old-fashioned jealousy that whipped through her. I won't succumb to another clutch of debilitating emotions, she told herself fiercely; it was bad enough being jealous of Fatima, without adding Janet Price to the list!

'You could say that,' was the taciturn reply, which did absolutely nothing to shift the green-eyed god of jealousy sitting on Harriet's shoulder. 'Next patient,' he called, signalling that the discussion was at an end, and with that Harriet had to be content.

Philippe worked alongside her for the rest of

the afternoon, and the clinic ran as smoothly as clockwork. Under normal circumstances Harriet would have enjoyed herself. The children were well-behaved, Philippe's presence had a calming effect on them, and the mothers were more co-operative. She should have been happy. But she couldn't rid herself of the feeling that she was walking along the edge of a precipice—one wrong word, and she'd slip into the abyss. Philippe might have had a calming effect on the patients, but Harriet found it was quite definitely the reverse on her!

He was infuriatingly polite. 'Ampoule, please,' he said every time he was ready to inject, then, 'Sugar lump, please.'

Although polite, by subtle tactics he had relegated her to the position of his handmaiden. He took over, and did everything that previously Harriet had been doing. All she was allowed to do was to wait on him!

He's paying me back for last night, thought Harriet. I *won't* let it get me down. 'Ampoule, sir,' she said, handing him the triple vaccine to go into the syringe.

His tanned hand brushed against hers, and he looked up. If he was surprised at her use of the word 'sir' he made no comment.

By the time the very last patient had gone, Harriet could stand the tension no longer. She knew she just had to apologise for her thoughtless words the previous night, but

Philippe's frigid politeness made her task unbearably difficult.

But from somewhere she dredged up the necessary courage, and stood rather shakily in front of him. 'I have something to say,' she began. Her voice trembled a little, betraying her nervousness.

'So it would seem.' Narrowing his eyes, he folded his arms and surveyed the slender girl before him.

There was a long silence, and any faint hope that Harriet had entertained of Philippe making it easier for her disappeared. He obviously wanted his pound of flesh. Gritting her teeth, she prepared to give it to him.

'I want to apologise for being so insulting last night. I shouldn't have said what I did, it was very wrong of me.'

'But, you thought it, nevertheless.'

'No, not really. The words just came out, because . . .' Philippe waited silently, still not endeavouring to help her out in the stumbling apology. Licking her lips nervously, Harriet continued in a hurry, before she lost what little courage she had left. 'It was because I wanted to hurt you. I blamed you for my betrayal of Felix. I punished you, when I should have punished myself.' Her voice sank to a whisper as she added, 'I'm sorry if I let you think by my actions that I . . .' she hesitated, 'that I was willing to get involved with you on a personal level. I shouldn't have done that. I'm not trying to excuse myself, and I don't blame you if you don't believe me when I tell you I've never behaved like that before. It is true, however. It must have been some kind of midsummer madness. It won't happen again.'

There, she had apologised, and told the most monumental lie into the bargain. Perhaps now she might be able to work with Philippe on a purely professional basis, and the passion she felt would die a natural death of its own accord. Perhaps, but the thought of working beside him for the next seventeen months stretched ahead like a life sentence of purgatory.

Without waiting for a reply Harriet turned to move away. But before she could move, a hand reached out and caught her shoulder. Slowly, but very deliberately, Philippe turned her back to face him.

'I owe you an apology, too,' he said in a low voice. 'I shouldn't have been self-indulgent. You see, I kissed you knowing full well that you were unhappy and vulnerable because Felix had gone away. However,' he paused and his dark face broke into a lop-sided smile, 'it is partly your own fault, Harriet.'

'My fault! Why?' Harriet looked up quickly, but then looked away again. She couldn't bring herself to look into those gleaming topaz eyes, or she would surely drown in their depths.

'Because you are much too attractive, Miss

Jones,' was Philippe's reply. Then he spoilt it by adding, matter-of-factly, 'We all have our weakness, and mine is a weakness for attractive women.'

'Oh, well,' Harriet attempted a light laugh, to match his faintly bantering tone, 'there are plenty of unattached attractive women around. Suzy, Janet and . . .' she stopped herself from saying Fatima, and finished lamely, 'and anyone else you fancy. Anyone, except me.' She looked at him, frowning. 'That brings me back to Felix. How did you know we broke your rules? And now that you do know, do you want me to go back to England?'

'Do you want to go back?'

'No,' she heard herself saying.

The next moment she was silently cursing herself for being a fool. He had given her the perfect opening, and she had refused it.

'In that case we might as well leave things as they are. I only stipulated unattached people because I didn't want any distractions. I wanted the full concentration of everyone for my hospital. Although,' he added thoughtfully, reaching forward and cupping her chin in his hand, 'I seem to have broken all my own rules where you are concerned.'

'A temporary lapse,' suggested Harriet, hastily backing away. His touch burned like fire on her skin.

It came almost as a disappointment to hear

him agree with her, as he shrugged his broad shoulders out of his white coat, and threw it on the couch.

'I'll give you the itinerary for the village clinics at dinner this evening,' he said, leaving the cubicle. From his tone of voice she knew he had put the matter from his mind and was already thinking of other things.

Left alone, she stood and watched his tall figure disappear rapidly down the long corridor. She had apologised, and so had he. And obviously, as far as he was concerned, that was the end of that.

But she still couldn't help wondering how he'd found out about her and Felix, he'd neatly skipped out of answering that question.

A bevy of cleaning ladies clattered down the corridor, brandishing their buckets and mops. They beamed at Harriet and surged forward enthusiastically to begin their task of washing everything in sight. Harriet smiled back, thinking how different they were from the cleaners at St James's. In London it was a constant battle to fish the cleaning ladies from the loos, where they were usually to be found having a crafty smoke. The actual job of cleaning came well down on their list of priorities.

Thoughts of St James's brought her back full circle to Felix. The sooner she told him of her decision to finish the engagement, the better. Then all she had to do was to work hard, and keep away from Philippe until it was time to return to England, and hopefully sanity!

It wasn't difficult keeping away from Philippe that evening, because Janet Price monopolised him the moment he appeared. It was obvious from their conversation that they knew each other well. It seemed there was no shortage of women in Philippe's life, past or present!

After the evening meal, Philippe offered to take Janet down into Bodrum. 'Great, I love exploring.' Janet looked pleased, and jumped up immediately. She turned to Harriet. 'Are you coming?'

'Well . . .' Harriet hesitated, unsure whether or not the invitation included her.

Philippe himself disposed of her doubts. 'No, Harriet has to work. The equipment and drugs needed for the village clinics tomorrow have to be collected together.' He fished a foolscap piece of paper out of his pocket as he spoke. 'Here is a list of villages, and beside each name is the approximate number of patients to be treated. So could you be sure to pack everything you will need into the minibus tonight? You will have to make an early start in the morning.'

Harriet took the neatly typed list he handed her. 'Yes, of course,' she said. Philippe had well and truly dismissed her. She had wanted their relationship to continue on a strictly business level, and so, evidently, did he. Why, then, didn't she feel pleased?

Janet didn't appear to notice anything untoward. 'Bad luck, Harriet,' she said sympathetically. 'Never mind, I expect this slave-driver will have me working every night next week.'

'Janet!' Philippe admonished her, playfully tugging at her luxuriant, chestnut-coloured ponytail. 'Anyone would think I had made you work hard in the past.'

'And didn't you just, you old bully?' said Janet, smiling at him affectionately. She slid an arm around his waist, in an unabashed, warm-hearted gesture, 'and you know how glad I was—eventually.'

Harriet turned away, as a wave of indescribable sadness swept over her. She wished it were possible for her to have that kind of relationship with Philippe, friendly, affectionate and open. She envied the friendship Janet and Philippe seemed to share, it was like that of a brother and sister.

A brother-sister relationship! her inner voice mocked her. Is that what you really want? No, what you really want is for Philippe to be your lover, to fulfil you as a woman!

She turned her attention to the list in her hand. 'Will you be able to manage all that?'

With a guilty start Harriet stared at Philippe. Heaven help her, if he could read her mind! 'Yes, of course,' she said hurriedly, 'don't worry about me.'

'I didn't intend to,' came the wry reply. 'Janet may be sorry for you, but I know you had your fun last night!'

Harriet felt her face flushing angrily.

'Oh.' Janet was filled with curiosity. 'This sounds exciting. Whatever did you do?'

'Went swimming in the harbour in the middle of the night,' said Harriet, and walked away. Let him get out of explaining that!

Loading the minibus with all the necessary items from the store room took the rest of the evening. Harriet checked and rechecked everything, determined that Philippe should not find a single thing wrong. By the time she'd finished she felt shattered, but staggered along to see Barry before she retreated to the peace of seraglio.

He was up when she arrived, and sitting outside his room in the cool. 'Hi,' she said, flopping into an armchair beside him.

'Hi.' He passed her a bottle of beer. 'I've eaten a huge supper and washed it down with beer,' he announced.

Harriet took a swig from the bottle. 'Wouldn't it have been better to have started off with a light supper, and some milk?' she enquired.

'Hell, no. I've been longing to get my teeth into some real food.' He leaned forward and flexed his muscles. 'I'm ready for anything tomorrow, my girl,' he boasted.

'Good,' said Harriet, 'because anything is

probably what we'll get!' She yawned. 'I'm going to bed. See you in the morning.'

Little did she know, as she climbed into bed, how prophetic her words would prove to be! She knew Suzy was already asleep, by the snores echoing loudly from her room. If the snores were anything to go by, Suzy seemed to have recovered from her bug already.

'I will not think of Philippe any more,' she said out loud, and closed her eyes.

But it seemed that the goats outside the window had other ideas. Every time she was very nearly asleep, they clanked their bells noisily, and the first picture to flash in front of her closed eyelids was of Philippe's darkly handsome face!

She finally succumbed to sleep with her face buried in the mattress, and the pillow firmly clasped over her ears to shut out the clanking goats' bells.

CHAPTER EIGHT

'DO YOU remember that awful breakfast we had on the first day?' Barry muttered thickly through a mouthful of bread and honey.

Harriet laughed. 'I certainly do, and yes, I *will* have some bread, before you demolish the lot!'

They were having breakfast alone, so that they could make their planned early start.

'It seems so long ago,' said Barry, echoing Harriet's own thoughts.

Harriet sighed; she felt restless and tired, probably due to those damned goats, she decided, with a flash of humour. Sipping scalding hot coffee, she gazed out from the terrace. The view of Bodrum Bay was strangely brilliant that morning. Everything stood out sharp-edged in the sunlight; it was also unbearably hot.

'I think a storm is coming,' she said, vainly attempting to fan herself with a napkin.

Even as Harriet spoke, the landscape began to darken, and a gargantuan black cloud billowed out from the mountain behind them. It covered the sky, blotting out the sun as it rolled out to sea.

Barry groaned. 'Surely it's not going to rain on my first day out,' he said in an aggrieved tone.

Harriet giggled at his outraged expression. 'There, there,' she teased, patting his hand. 'I won't let you get wet. I've booked the minibus, we're not going by camel!'

Two hours later, alone in the rain, with only an ineffectual piece of plastic sheeting to shield her as she ran towards a village house, she remembered her lack of sympathy for Barry.

'How prophetic,' she muttered under her breath, 'I must have known instinctively that he'd be all right! He's not getting wet, I am!'

Barry was still at the hospital, dealing with an emergency, and Harriet had come out alone. The minibus had been on the point of actually driving through the archway when they had very nearly collided with a decrepit lorry which chugged doggedly past them into the courtyard, followed by Philippe in his jeep. In the back of the lorry was a youngish man in a semi-conscious state. Neither Barry nor Harriet needed Philippe to tell them the man was suffering from life-threatening tachyarrhythmia, a brief physical examination had soon determined that.

'Resus,' snapped Philippe as soon as they were in the casualty-room.

Harriet set up the resuscitation equipment and helped Philippe put an intravenous cannula in situ, while Barry rushed along to the surgical ward to get the defibrillator.

'Damn,' Philippe cursed under his breath. 'We shouldn't have put it on the ward. There's no time to lose, his level of consciousness is beginning to change, and he has circulatory failure.'

'Hurry up, Barry,' said Harriet under her breath.

They were both oblivious of the crowd of anxious relatives, crowding in the doorway of the room. Harriet clamped an oxygen mask over the patient's face and applied a sixty per cent concentration of oxygen, while Philippe proceeded to give IV diazepam.

Barry returned, defibrillator rattling along on its trolley beside him. He glanced at the patient, and the slowly filtering diazepam. 'Maybe we won't have to use the defibrillator after all,' he said hopefully.

But as he spoke the ECG showed the patient sliding into deep unconsciousness. 'He's going to arrest,' said Harriet urgently.

'Don't I bloody know it,' muttered Barry.

'Get rid of those relatives, Harriet,' barked Philippe, 'while we put the defib paddles on.'

Harriet walked as calmly as she could towards the anxious crowd. Smiling a gentle, but her most fiercely professional, smile, she shut the door very firmly behind her, and ushered them along the corridor into another room. By sign language, she made it clear that this was where they were to stay for the time being.

At least, she kept her fingers crossed and hoped they had understood her. The last thing these gentle, unsophisticated people needed to see was a cardiac arrest, especially if Philippe and Barry were unable to save the patient. Let him be all right, she whispered under her breath. The straight line on the electrocardiograph, and the accompanying high-pitched whistle, always depressed Harriet. Death was something she had never become immune to, even though, as a nurse, she had witnessed it many times.

Back in the casualty-room, the paddles were fixed in place on the patient. Harriet saw that he hadn't yet arrested, but the monitor was all over the place—it was a question of time.

'I'm going to shock him,' Philippe said to Barry as she entered. 'Stand back and fire when I tell you.'

Harriet stood well out of the way, while Philippe held on to the rubber handles of the paddles, watching the ECG monitor carefully.

'Now,' he said.

With the defibrillator on the synchronized mode, Barry kept the firing button depressed until the synchronization mechanism allowed the shock to coincide with the correct wave of the ECG monitor. He timed it perfectly—a shock came at exactly the right time, and after a few seconds of intense electrical activity, a stable rhythm returned to the screen.

The three of them simultaneously let out their breaths in a long whistle of satisfaction. 'Thank heavens for modern technology,' said Harriet softly, watching the comforting regular pattern, blip-blipping on the monitor screen.

'Yep,' agreed Barry, helping Philippe remove the paddles from the patient's chest, 'this chap sure would have been a goner if he had arrived here any later.'

On Philippe's instructions, Harriet found Sofi, and asked her to explain to the relatives that they would have to wait a while longer before seeing their loved one. 'But hopefully, not too long,' she said.

Sofi sped off on her mission, and Harriet returned to the casualty-reception room.

By then an hour had elapsed since she and Barry had attempted to set off for the villages. 'I'd better start out on my own,' suggested Harriet, 'otherwise they will never get done.'

'I agree,' said Barry. 'OK if I use your jeep to catch up with her later?' He looked at Philippe.

'Yes,' he said, but he was looking distracted.

'Is there another problem?' asked Harriet, wondering what was worrying him.

Philippe looked at the ventilator which had been brought along from intensive care. The sound of the pumping bellows filled the room with a comforting rhythm. 'I was thinking,' he said slowly, 'if the locals are going to start using this place as a casualty unit—and after today, when the word gets around, they almost certainly will—we ought to have another ventilator and defibrillator.'

'Mention it to Fatima,' said Barry, 'she'll buy them.'

'It must be wonderful to be Lady Bountiful,' said Harriet under her breath.

Barry heard her and stared at her in surprise. 'As she's got pots of money,' he said quietly, 'it might as well be put to good use.'

'I know, I know,' Harriet felt guilty. 'It was a bitchy thing to say.' She turned to go. 'I'll see you later, then.'

'Yes,' said Barry, still looking at her with a puzzled expression.

Harriet wished she could feel more charitable towards Fatima, but it was no use. Every time she thought of Fatima, unwelcome thoughts of Philippe followed close behind, and that only served to depress her. But she couldn't very well tell Barry that!

Now, staggering through the mud, supplies under one arm, the other hand holding flimsy plastic sheeting over her head, uncharitable thoughts concerning Fatima had long since disappeared. Treacherous mudslides had made the journey through the mountains hazardous, but Harriet's mind had been less occupied with her own safety than with the abject poverty she had seen in the villages they'd passed through. The torrential rain made the wretched life of the mountain inhabitants virtually intolerable, and she began to understand more and more why Philippe had a passionate desire to help these people.

In spite of her sarcastic remark about 'Lady Bountiful', she knew Fatima's money would be well spent. Because for all her nursing skills, Harriet knew she, and others like her, could only make a small dent here and there in the lives of the mountain people. But with Fatima's money, the health education programme Philippe had planned could go ahead, and major changes would be made. It was wrong and stupid to resent Fatima and her money.

Harriet entered the village house, which, according to Ali, was where the first clinic was due to be set up. Looking around, she could see from even the most cursory of glances that the conditions could not be described as hygienic. Not by any figment of the imagination! Harriet wished she had another nurse with her to help out; there was so much to do it almost overwhelmed her.

To her surprise, however, Ali proved to be a willing helper.

'I must scrub the table and sink with disinfectant before we start,' she told him, preparing to do it herself.

'No!' Ali was quite firm. 'I do. Dr Krir said to help.' He pushed Harriet out of the way and started scrubbing vigorously, even though by his puzzled glances Harriet could tell he thought her rather eccentric!

'Thank you, Ali,' said Harriet gratefully when he'd finished. 'Now I'll just put this on, and then we're ready to start.' She spread clean plastic sheeting over the table which was to be used as a couch.

Ali ushered the first patients into the little house, and Harriet started her immunisation clinic. Somehow in the next hour and a half Harriet managed to immunise all the small patients shepherded in by their anxious mothers.

Recognised psychological theories drummed into her on paediatric courses, concerning the establishment of a rapport with children and mothers, went out of the window. Along with many other procedures which would have been considered essential in an English hospital.

In-depth conversation was an impossibility due to the language barrier, but Ali more than compensated. He proved to be an expert, although somewhat unorthodox, in mime language, and Harriet found herself giggling along with the children as he demonstrated his quite unique skills. Between them, and with the aid of her dog-eared dictionary, they succeeded in keeping everyone happy, and getting the job done.

As the last patient left, Ali turned to Harriet. 'Is finished,' he said. 'Now, we go?'

'Now, we go,' Harriet confirmed, and pointed to the name of the next village on her list.

It was with an exhilarating sense of achievement that they drove out of the village. The rain had stopped and, undeterred by the ankle-deep mud, the entire village turned out to wave them goodbye. A sea of small brown arms, each with a prominent sticking plaster—their badges of courage, thought Harriet fondly—was the last thing she saw as they rounded the corner of the mountainside, and started off again on their journey.

Harriet had the map on her lap. 'Where is it?' she asked, peering at the unfamiliar names.

'Is here.' Ali's fat brown finger stabbed at the map. 'Don't worry, I know.'

The route was through a series of hairpin bends. The view alternated at every bend, a sheer drop down to the sea one moment, followed by the solid granite wall of the mountain the next. Harriet began to relax, happy to let Ali take the strain, when the minibus suddenly skidded, and Ali slumped over the wheel. In the fraction of a second that it

NEW BEGINNINGS

happened, Harriet's brain registered that not only was Ali ill, but that they were about to roar off into space from the edge of the next sheer drop.

Quick as a flash, she leaned over and, summoning up superhuman strength, wrenched at the wheel and handbrake for all she was worth. It seemed a terrifyingly long time before anything happened, then the bus veered away from the edge, and ground to a shuddering halt.

Harriet jumped out and ran round to the driver's side, intent on dragging Ali out so that she could help him. But as she reached the front of the cab she stopped, gasping in horror. Oh, no, she hadn't managed to turn the wheel enough! Disaster had only been averted by a hair's breadth, the driver's wheel was half over the edge. With a gulp of fear, Harriet realised that it only needed a couple of inches of the rain-sodden earth to give way, and the minibus would roll down the mountainside.

A village bus rounded the corner and screeched to a halt just in time to avoid crashing into the periously poised bus. The occupants tumbled out and milled helplessly around Harriet. 'A rope,' she called to them, desperately trying to mime what she wanted, 'I want a rope.'

The driver understood and, running round to

the side luggage compartment, produced a length of rope. It was strong and a reasonable length, and Harriet began to tie one end around her waist.

A second screech of brakes announced the arrival of another vehicle, but Harriet didn't bother to look up, she was too preoccupied. 'What the hell is going on?'

At the familiar voice Harriet looked up almost bursting into tears of relief. Her unspoken prayers for help had been answered, for a sort of divine providence must have brought Philippe up the mountainside at that precise moment. 'Ali has had either a heart attack or a stroke,' she stuttered, the words tumbling one over the other. 'We nearly went over the edge.'

'I can see that! What the hell is that for?' He indicated the rope, by now tied tightly around Harriet's slim waist.

'I'm going to drag him out of the cab. Now you're here, if you could get some of these people to hold the . . .'

'You'll do no such thing,' said Philippe harshly. 'That bus could go over the edge any minute.'

'I know,' cried Harriet, 'that's why I've got to get Ali out now, there's no time to lose.'

'I can't let you do it. You could be killed.'

'So could Ali,' said Harriet. 'Oh, Philippe, we can't leave him there to die, either from lack of treatment, or by crashing down the mountain in the bus. Please help me.'

'Untie that rope,' said Philippe, throwing off his jacket. 'I'll go.'

Harriet shook her head stubbornly. 'No, you're too big and too heavy, your weight would definitely tip the bus over. It *has* to be me, you know that.'

After a split-second hesitation, Philippe nodded his head. 'You're right,' he said, 'but I wish you weren't.' He shouted something to the crowd in Turkish, and another rope was produced. He gave the end to Harriet. 'Tie this around Ali, under his armpits. Don't attempt to pull him yourself. That's an order! When you've tied it, slide back out, and we will pull Ali.'

Harriet took the rope in her hand, and prepared to climb into the front of the bus. 'OK, here goes,' she said.

Irrationally, she felt that everything was sure to turn out all right now that Philippe had arrived. Even though Ali must be seriously ill, and the bus might still topple over the edge any moment, they'd both be all right, because Philippe would see they were safe. She started to climb aboard the bus.

'Harriet, for heaven's sake take care, don't move so quickly. Do everything in slow motion.'

Philippe's voice was hoarse.

Their eyes met for a brief moment, and Harriet saw that beneath his tan his face was pale and anxious. She slowed down, trying to make her movements as smooth as possible, and wishing she felt braver. I'm not cut out for heroics, she thought, as she said, 'I'll be careful.'

As she clambered further in, the minibus began to sway. Perspiration trickled down her forehead, and Harriet felt breathless. 'I've got to get Ali out, I've got to get Ali out.' She repeated the words aloud softly time and time again, as slowly, inch by inch, she wound the rope around Ali's inert body. He was still alive, she could feel a weak pulse, but it was very difficult trying to move him. He was completely unconscious, and a dead weight.

Suddenly, the bus swayed violently, Harriet held her breath, but let it out with a sigh as the bus settled back down again with a crunch. Determinedly she fought back the nausea that threatened to engulf her, and tried not to look at the sea glittering menacingly far below. It seemed hours before she had the ends securely fastened, and had managed to twist Ali's body around so that it could be pulled from the cab without injuring him further.

'You can start to pull now,' she called back to Philippe, who was hovering as near as possible to the door of the bus.

'No, you get out first,' came the terse reply. 'Ease yourself backwards; we'll help by pulling on the rope.' His strong hands grasped her waist, and lifted her bodily from the cab as soon as she was within reach. 'Thank heavens,' he said, briefly brushing her cheek with his hand, before turning away.

Harriet, her feet now on solid ground, watched as Philippe directed the rescue operation for Ali. Slowly and carefully, the willing crowd pulled on the rope, inching his unconscious body towards safety. As soon as his head and shoulders reached the door, willing hands pulled Ali out.

Within seconds, both she and Philippe were on their knees in the mud of the road beside Ali. 'He was already cyanosed when I first got to him,' said Harriet. The blueness of Ali's lips showed through his tan. She picked up his hand; the fingernails were blue too.

Philippe nodded, and pushed his stethoscope back in his pocket. 'I'm pretty sure it's a massive heart attack. We'll put him in my jeep and get him back down to the hospital. There's nothing we can do here without equipment.'

On the way back, Harriet crouched in the rear of the jeep with the unconscious Ali. She kept her fingers over his fluttering pulse, willing it to keep going. Philippe drove as fast as was humanly possible, but they both knew time and the terrain were against them. The journey seemed agonisingly slow, and Harriet could feel the pulse beneath her fingertips growing weaker and more irregular by the minute.

She looked down at Ali. It hardly seemed possible that this was the lively man who had made those children so happy just a few short hours ago. Now he was near to death, and she prayed that they would reach the hospital in time to help him. But as the jeep started the ascent towards the hospital, and the stark outlines of the palace rose before them into the sky, Ali's pulse finally ebbed away, and there was nothing.

Her mind switched into gear. Not allowing herself to think, and on automatic pilot, Harriet did all the things she had been taught. Mouth to mouth resuscitation, followed by chest massage; two breaths to fifteen presses, one and . . . two and . . . three and . . . Harriet counted and kept an eye on her watch. After one minute, she checked the carotid pulse; there was no sign of a heartbeat, so she continued with the resuscitation attempt, hoping against hope that the heart would start up again.

When Philippe opened the back doors of the jeep in the courtyard, all Harriet could do was to shake her head despairingly.

She helped Barry and Philippe carry on with the resuscitation attempt, now using all the equipment available. But Harriet instinctively felt it was hopeless and, seeing the anguished expression blazing from Philippe's eyes, she knew he thought the same. When he finally announced defeat, his voice was low with emotion. Harriet dashed the moistness from her eyes with a swift movement; it would never do to cry. Nurses didn't cry.

'It happens,' said Barry, seeing Harriet's hand movement and her stricken expression. 'We won this morning, and lost this afternoon. You know we can never win them all.'

'I know,' she said wanly.

Then, before she disgraced herself in front of them by actually bursting into tears, Harriet turned and ran. She didn't stop running until she'd reached the haven of her room in the seraglio. Only then did she fling herself on the bed and cry bitter tears of regret and sorrow. Why weren't they given more time, why did they have to be so far from the hospital?

'Why, why, why?' She sobbed the words out loud.

'Because that is the way of life—and death,' said a voice quietly. 'None of us is immortal, not even you or I.'

'I know that, but . . .' Without thinking, she buried her face against the comforting warmth of his chest and let the tears flood, unchecked. Philippe held her close, stroking her hair gently, as he might have done to a distraught child.

It was only when Harriet's sobs subsided that he put her away from him and, fishing out a snow white handkerchief from his pocket, passed it to her.

'Thank you.' Harriet took the proffered handkerchief, and attempted to wipe away the ravages of her tears. 'I'm sorry,' she muttered, suddenly feeling embarrassed, 'I shouldn't have lost control like that. But I . . . I had become very fond of Ali.'

'So was I,' replied Philippe, 'but there is something that perhaps you should know. Ali was living on borrowed time. He knew that and so did his family. Two years ago he had a heart attack, a very bad one. He wouldn't take my advice to give up smoking; it was only a matter of time before something happened again.' He sighed. 'Although I thought he would develop severe angina, not have a massive coronary. If I'd even thought——' Suddenly, he pulled Harriet back into his arms. 'I should never have let him drive,' he whispered. 'If that bus had gone over the edge . . . I can't even bear to think about it.'

His heart was beating like a sledge-hammer, and Harriet's lips curved into the beginnings of a tremulous smile as she listened to the thundering sound. 'Would it have mattered?' she whispered, looking up at him through tear-stained lashes. 'I mean mattered to——'

'Harriet!' Felix's voice echoed down the corridor as he called, accompanied by the sound of running feet.

'It would have mattered a lot to Felix,' said Philippe, suddenly releasing her from his arms and standing up. 'I'm sure he prefers his fiancée alive!' He turned and called towards the door, 'Harriet is in here, Felix.' Turning back, he surveyed the tear-blotched face, and mud-stained clothes. 'I came to warn you of Felix's arrival,' he said, 'because I thought you'd prefer to change before you saw him, but he has beaten me to it.'

Harriet watched his lithe form cross the room towards the door. She had been foolish enough to think that he had come because he cared about her. Oh, why hadn't he come for her?

Felix brushed past Philippe in the doorway, 'Harriet!' he exclaimed. 'Everyone is talking about your heroic rescue; apparently you were marvellous!'

'Heroic rescue!' echoed Harriet, her voice harsh and bitter. 'But didn't Philippe tell you? It was all a waste of time. Ali died anyway.'

She watched Philippe cross the courtyard and disappear from view while Felix talked, but his words fell on deaf ears. Complete and utter misery at her failure on all fronts overwhelmed her.

CHAPTER NINE

FELIX blustered and protested when Harriet first told him of her wish to formally break the engagement. She couldn't decide whether to be sad or amused when she saw that, in spite of his protestations, he wasn't exactly heart-broken.

'Well, at least no one knows,' he said eventually, 'so there'll be no loss of face.'

'Whose face?' murmured Harriet wryly.

Felix looked slightly awkward. 'You know what I mean. A man doesn't like to be ditched.'

'Better than being unhappily married,' said Harriet. 'Surely you agree?'

'I'll have to think of something to tell the folks back in England.'

'You could always tell them the truth,' snapped Harriet tartly. 'Just say we found we weren't suited.'

It was typical of Felix to consider outward appearances as vitally important. To Harriet, that was the least important part of all. She was tempted for a moment to tell him that somehow

Philippe had known, but then decided to hold her tongue. Philippe could go on thinking they were secretly engaged—that way her fragile barrier of self-defence could remain intact.

The next few weeks following Ali's death seemed curiously empty to Harriet, although she couldn't think why. New equipment arrived at the hospital daily, and the workload increased as more patients were admitted on to both the medical and surgical wards. Soon the three English girls found themselves acting as nurse tutors to a new batch of Turkish girls Philippe had recruited.

Now in the evening the seraglio was noisy, echoing to the laughing chatter of more than two dozen voices. This is how it must have been in the ancient days, thought Harriet, sitting by the pool one evening, trailing her fingers in the cooling water.

She was thinking about Philippe, something she tried not to do. But tonight she couldn't help wondering where he was, and what he was doing. He had been away with Fatima for nearly two weeks now.

'I bet they're buying up half of Europe,' said Janet with a laugh, almost as if she could read Harriet's thoughts.

She and Suzy came and sat beside Harriet, continuing their gossip about Philippe and Fatima. By now, everyone knew that Janet was a widow too. According to her, she had gone to pieces after her husband's death, and Philippe had picked up the pieces and glued her together. His remedy had been to propel her back into nursing, making her work so hard she hadn't found time to grieve.

'Yes, well, of course Fatima is . . .'

Harriet left the poolside and returned to her room the moment she heard Fatima's name mentioned. She was gradually managing to draw down the shutters of her mind where Philippe was concerned, and didn't want to be reminded of him. Whenever the conversation turned to Philippe or Fatima, she either deflected the talk to another subject, or left the room. It was a poor defence, she knew, but it was the only one she had.

The following week they were due to return from their travels, and then Harriet knew she'd have to work out some other strategy. She couldn't shut her ears and eyes to their actual presence!

The day before Philippe and Fatima were due to arrive back in Turkey, there was great excitement. Madame Krir issued a personal invitation to all the off-duty staff of the hospital to attend a barbecue party in the garden of Philippe's villa. Harriet gazed down at her own invitation card with dismay. She didn't want to go back to the villa with all its memories, and she wanted to put off coming face to face with

Philippe for as long as possible. To make matters worse, Madame Krir had even added a little handwritten note to her invitation, saying how much she was looking forward to meeting Harriet again!

That evening, the seraglio was fairly bursting with noise, as all the girls swapped notes on what they were doing.

'Just my luck, to be on duty,' Suzy grumbled to Harriet. 'This is the first party since we've been here.'

'What a shame,' Harriet commiserated, suddenly seeing a golden opportunity for getting out of the barbecue.

When the next evening arrived, Harriet decided to develop a headache and nausea. She went along to see Suzy who was moping around, bemoaning the fact she was still in uniform when everyone else was glamorous!

'Get changed,' said Harriet. 'I'll stay and do your duty.'

'Oh, but you can't, that wouldn't be fair,' protested Suzy.

'Yes it is. There's no point in me going when I feel sick, and I know I've got this thumping headache coming on.'

'Oh . . .' Suzy began to weaken. 'All you'd have to do is to supervise the four Turkish girls working on the newly opened wards.'

'I know, I can manage that even with a headache,' Harriet said. 'Go on, you go.

Look, I've even written a note to Madame Krir, explaining my absence and your presence.' She passed a sealed envelope to Suzy.

'Well . . . if you're sure.'

'I am,' said Harriet.

Suzy stopped protesting immediately, in case Harriet should change her mind. 'OK,' she said, grinning from ear to ear at the prospect of the barbecue. 'The patients shouldn't give you any problems. They're quite well really. Barry has been over-cautious in keeping them in. The girls are perfectly competent. Once round with the lamp, Florence Nightingale, and then you can go to bed! What do you think I ought to wear, my blue or red trousers?'

'Blue,' said Harriet.

Harriet walked to the main courtyard and watched them depart.

Suzy appeared, poured into the red trousers. She saw Harriet's glance. 'I know, I know, the blue are better. But I've put on weight and couldn't even get the zip done up on those.'

'With any luck, you'll burst out of these before the evening's out,' said Barry, smacking her on the behind.

'Keep your hands to yourself, Dr South,' snapped Suzy, attempting a dignified entrance into the minibus. 'Oh, hell, I can't bend my knees. Help me, Barry!'

Harriet started laughing as Barry hauled a

furiously blushing Suzy up the steps and into the bus. Eventually everyone was squeezed in, like so many sardines. Even Felix had accepted the invitation, Harriet noticed, and appeared to be getting on very well with Janet Price.

The palace seemed very lonely when the sounds of excited laughter had died away. The last call of the day came from the muezzin drifted up from the mosque in Bodrum. The sound echoed from every corner, emphasising the emptiness. Harriet walked slowly across the courtyard, through the pools of warm moonlight, and made her way down the long corridors towards the wards.

Suzy's forecast had been right. The patients, two children and two adults, were very well. The new nurses were happily bustling about serving the supper, before sitting down to their own.

'Anything I can do?'

'No, no, Miss Harriet,' the girls chorused in unison, obviously anxious to get rid of her and resume overall charge once more.

Harriet felt superfluous; they didn't need her and were not likely to. Oh, well, she'd done her Florence Nightingale bit as Suzy had said; now she could go back to the seraglio.

Completely on her own for once, she decided to make full use of the Hammam. Once this had been a full-blown Turkish bath, with steamrooms, cold-rooms, and massage-room. Now, it had been converted into a series of spectacular bathrooms, although the old name had been retained.

An hour later, her skin smooth and perfumed, Harriet put on the silk robe she had bought that week in the Kale Cad market. The deep rose pinks and reds of the material set off her golden skin to perfection. The material fell in graceful, sleek folds around the shape of her body—a pity, she thought, idly regarding her reflection in the mirror, that there's no one to appreciate it!

C'est la vie! Taking some cushions and a book, she crossed the bridge and sat in the cool of the gazebo and gazed at the smooth waters of the lake.

If this was three hundred years ago, I would be awaiting the arrival of my lover, she thought wryly. But it was here and now, and she didn't have a lover, she was alone. With a sigh, she switched on the gazebo's hanging lantern, and settled down on the cushions to read.

'Harriet.' Philippe's voice came out of the darkness as he crossed the arched bridge spanning the water to the gazebo.

The book slid from her nerveless fingers as Harriet scrambled to her feet. 'What are you doing here?' she whispered.

'What all men have done down the centuries in this place!' he said. 'I've come for the woman

I want.' He held out his arms. 'Come to me,' he said.

'Philippe.'

It was a sigh as much as a word. Harriet swayed towards him, revelling in the lovely agony as his fingers closed around her slender waist, the pressure piercing through the thin silk of her robe.

'I love you, Harriet.' He was speaking the words she had never thought to hear, his voice husky with emotion. 'I've loved you since the first day I saw you, and I was determined to get you here.' He saw her questioning look. 'Yes, I knew then you were engaged to Felix, one of the other surgeons let the cat out of the bag! But one look at you and I broke my rules, and I've gone on breaking them ever since.'

Then his mouth closed over hers in a kiss. Now there was no doubt of the strength of his feelings. With infinite mastery, and very, very gently Philippe laid her back down among the cushions, and covered her body with his.

When at last he lifted his head, Harriet was trembling with desire, but somehow she still managed to cling on to reality, there was something she had to know.

'What about Fatima?' she forced herself to say. 'Is this fair to her?'

Her words succeeded in stopping Philippe dead in his tracks. 'Fatima!' he said, raising himself on one elbow, and staring down at her. 'What the hell has this got to do with Fatima?'

'But aren't you going to marry her? Your mother told you to pay her more attention, I thought——'

Philippe started to laugh—a low, deep chuckle that blossomed into a full-bellied shout of laughter. A frog sitting peacefully on a lily pad took fright, and jumped into the water with a splash. When he'd managed to control his laughter, Philippe turned his full attention back to Harriet.

'Fatima, my darling,' he said in between kisses, 'is my sister. I thought you knew.' He shook his head in wonderment. 'Surely you heard Janet talking about her? She and Fatima are great friends now. They are both widows, and they met when they worked for me in England. That's why Janet always teases me about being a slave-driver.'

'Yes, I know about Janet, but she never said . . . I never guessed——'

'Perhaps you weren't listening. Anyway, it doesn't matter now. Actually, it's because of Janet that I'm here.'

'Oh?' Harriet was mystified.

'Janet was flirting madly with Felix at the barbecue. So I interfered as usual, and took him on one side. I told him in no uncertain terms that he should remember his fiancée back at the hospital. I couldn't bear to think of you being hurt. It was then that he told me you had broken it off.' Philippe cupped his hands around her face. 'Why did you let me go on thinking you were still engaged?' he asked softly.

'Because of you and Fatima,' said Harriet. 'I had my pride. I didn't want to make a fool of myself.' Then she added ruefully, 'Oh, what a waste of time.'

'At last I'm beginning to understand the ''stop—go'' signals I was receiving. You had me thoroughly confused, but tonight, when I found out you were free, I knew I had to chance it. I had to tell you how I really felt.'

'I'm so glad you did.' Harriet traced the outline of his jaw with one finger. 'Otherwise we might still be wasting time.'

'Exactly,' said Philippe, beginning to kiss her again. 'We have a lot of time to make up.'

'I love you, Philippe.' In between kisses, Harriet tried out the words she had been longing to say for so long. 'I love you, I love you.'

'You'll marry me,' he said. 'As soon as it can be arranged.'

Harriet smiled; he hadn't asked, he had commanded. But it didn't matter, for once she didn't want to feel the least bit emancipated. 'Yes,' she said, adding softly, 'my lord and master.'

NEW BEGINNINGS

For a long moment they lay gazing into each other's eyes. Then slowly Philippe slid the silken robe aside, until the lamplight gleamed on the delicate curves of her body. With reverence, his warm hand closed over the soft mound of her breast.

'I told you that if you waited long enough in the seraglio, the right man would come.'

Hello!

As a reader, you may not have thought about trying to write a book yourself, but if you have, and you have a particular interest in medicine, then now is your chance.

We are specifically looking for new writers to join our established team of authors who write Medical Romances. Guidelines are available for this list, and we would be happy to send them to you.

Please mark the outside of your envelope 'Medical' to help speed our response, and we would be most grateful if you could include a stamped self-addressed envelope, size approximately $9\frac{1}{4}"$ x $4\frac{3}{4}"$, sent to the address below.

We look forward to hearing from you.

Editorial Department,
Mills & Boon Limited,
Eton House,
18-24 Paradise Road,
Richmond, Surrey,
TW9 1SR.

THE IDEAL TONIC

Over the past year, we have listened carefully to readers' comments, and so, in August, Mills & Boon are launching a *new look* Doctor-Nurse series – MEDICAL ROMANCES.

There will still be three books every month from a wide selection of your favourite authors. As a special bonus, the three books in August will have a special offer price of **ONLY** 99p each.

So don't miss out on this chance to get a real insight into the fast-moving and varied world of modern medicine, which gives such a unique background to drama, emotions – and romance!

Widely available from Boots, Martins, John Menzies, W.H. Smith, Woolworths and other paperback stockists.
Usual price £1.25

THE COMPELLING AND UNFORGETTABLE SAGA OF THE CALVERT FAMILY

April	August	November
£2.95	£3.50	£3.50

From the American Civil War to the outbreak of World War I, this sweeping historical romance trilogy depicts three generations of the formidable and captivating Calvert women – Sarah, Elizabeth and Catherine.

The ravages of war, the continued divide of North and South, success and failure, drive them all to discover an inner strength which proves they are true Calverts.

Top author Maura Seger weaves passion, pride, ambition and love into each story, to create a set of magnificent and unforgettable novels.

W✿RLDWIDE

Widely available on dates shown from Boots, Martins, John Menzies, W.H. Smith, Woolworths and other paperback stockists.